Transports and Disgraces

ILLINOIS SHORT FICTION

Transports and Disgraces

Stories by
Robert Henson

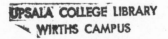
UNIVERSITY OF ILLINOIS PRESS

Urbana   Chicago   London

"Billie Loses Her Job," *Antioch Review,* vol. 37, no. 1, Winter 1979

"The Upper and the Lower Millstone," *Eureka Review,* Winter 1975/76; third prize winner in *O. Henry Prize Stories 1978*

"The Education of Michael Wigglesworth," *Transatlantic Review,* Spring/Summer 1972

"Lykaon," *Epoch,* Winter 1969; reprinted in *Best Little Magazine Fiction: 1970*

"Lizzie Borden in the P.M.," *Quarterly Review of Literature,* Spring/Summer 1973; second prize winner in *O. Henry Prize Stories 1974;* reprinted in *QRL 30th Anniversary Prose Retrospective, 1975*

Library of Congress Cataloging in Publication Data

Henson, Robert, 1921-
    Transports and disgraces.

    (Illinois short fiction)
    CONTENTS: Billie loses her job.—The upper and
lower millstone.—The education of Michael
Wigglesworth.—[etc.]
    I. Title.
PZ4.H5258Tr [PS3558.E57]   813'.54   80-19131
ISBN   0-252-00840-5 (cloth)
ISBN   0-252-00841-3 (paper)

For Tasia Wolf

The Past is such a curious Creature
To look her in the Face
A Transport may receipt us
Or a Disgrace—

Unarmed if any meet her
I charge him fly
Her faded Ammunition
Might yet reply.

—Emily Dickinson

Contents

Billie Loses Her Job

When I came out of prison in 1936, a man named Jax was waiting at the gate to sign me up for a personal appearance tour with his carnival: "Jax Shows—Pre-eminent in the Field."

I said I didn't have nothing to tell. "Besides," I said, "he's been dead two years."

"Oh Billie," he said, "if I could just show you the newspaper clippings, the magazine articles, even the movies! Ever hear of this new guy, Humphrey Bogart?—it's him right down to the grin! What's the biggest draw at the FBI in Washington, D.C.?—his .38, the straw hat he was wearing, his sunglasses. John Dillinger's a legend, Billie, an American hero!"

I said it was news to me.

"The lodge where him and the FBI shot it out—Little Bohemia, remember?—that guy's got a gold mine, tourists beating a path up there just to look at the bullet holes!"

"I wasn't there," I said. "That's what I mean."

I was going to Neopit, Wisconsin, to visit my mother, then on to Chicago to find work. Inside I'd learned how to *do* something for the first time in my life, even if it was only cutting shirtwaist patterns. My supervisor told the parole board I was the best worker she ever had. But . . . outside it was still hard times—especially for women, Indians, and ex-cons. How'd you like to be all three? When Mr. Jax looked me up again several months later, I'd left Chicago. I was back in Neopit.

He didn't have the look white men usually had when they knocked on a door on the reservation. He said, "I knew I was in the right place as soon as I saw that tepee." He meant the fake tepee refreshment stand for tourists that was in the middle of town. Indians were just show business to him.

"Actually I'm only half Menominee," I told him. "Of course, it's the half that shows."

"You got a nice smile, Billie," he said. "You got beautiful eyes. I still want you to join the midway. People'd take to you if you didn't do nothing but smile and say, Hello, I'm Billie Frechette. Crowds are one thing I *know* about."

They'd been playing lots in Illinois for a month and were fixing to loop down through Missouri, Kansas, and Oklahoma. "If you joined us now you'd have a whole month before we start hitting the fairs and the big crowds. However," he said, "in case you're still hesitating, I've got this great big ace up my sleeve. Guess who you'll be on the platform with? John Dillinger *Senior!* Just signed!"

I couldn't think of what to say. We were sitting at the kitchen table, wind blowing straight through the house from front to back. My mother never closed a window from June to November. Mr. Jax looked at the wall behind me where there was an old calendar picture of Lindbergh in his aviator's cap.

"An American hero, Billie, just like Lindy!"

"I've met Mr. Dillinger," I said.

"All the better! Did you know he started going out two weeks after Johnny was killed! Vaudeville, midways, he's even given talks at Little Bohemia. Don't that tell you something? But *this*—his dad and his only true love on the same bill! We'll pack 'em in! Don't get me wrong," he said. "This here'll be an office attraction—that means my own personal management. It won't be no freak show, I promise you."

I wasn't thinking about that.

Sure enough, before we ever got to the fair dates, he called me in for a talk. "Billie, Billie, Billie," he says, shaking his head, "you could go down in history as the *one woman* in John Dillinger's life. But you know what's gonna happen? The Woman in Red's gonna take your place. Not the woman that stuck by him, but the one that sold him out! How could you let that happen?

"I'm gonna have to let you go, Billie," he says.

The way he used to shake his head, and say my name over always reminded me of Louis Piquett, Johnny's mouthpiece. "Billie, Billie, Billie," he'd say, "Johnny wants to *marry* you! Doesn't that mean anything to you?"

Well, he wanted to marry me as soon as he met me. I was working hat check in a nightclub in Chicago. The first time he come in he leaned across the counter and said, "Know something?—you got beautiful eyes." The next two nights we had drinks on my break. He said he was from Indianapolis and had to go back on business but he'd send for me if I'd come.

"What kind of business?"

He opened his billfold and took out some clippings from Indiana newspapers, all about a daring new bank robber who'd walked in with a straw hat tipped over one eye, announced a stickup and then—instead of pushing open the teller's door—jumped up on the ledge and vaulted right over the cage.

"Why'd you do that?" I asked.

He said he didn't know why, he didn't even think about it—"All at once I was just flying through the air. Will you come if I send for you? I know we've just met but, baby, I've fallen for you in a great big way. Say razzberries, but to me that means just one thing. I want to be with you forever. . . ."

He always did talk like a popular song. It wasn't what he *said* that made me go to Indianapolis a few months later. In fact, I told him right off that I was married and couldn't get a divorce because my husband had been sent up for fifteen years and I didn't know where. He gave Louis Piquett a standing order: "Find the louse."

Louis had contacts in every pen in the forty-eight states, but finding Sparks wasn't that easy. He told me in private it was hard to believe I didn't know where my own husband had been sent.

I said, "Well, he wasn't tried in Chicago, it was in St. Louis. So I couldn't be there."

"And he never *once* got in touch with you after he was sentenced?"
"I guess he was ashamed."

When I first met the man I married, I asked why everyone called him Sparks instead of George. He said it was because he was an electrician.

I was crazy about baseball in those days. On Saturdays I used to hitch a ride into Shawano with my girlfriend. Usually we'd just stand around, but if there was a baseball game that's where I'd be. He turned up one summer playing first base for the Shawano team. He was Menominee but he'd gone away to Haskell Indian School in Kansas, then did odd jobs around the country.

He took me to Chicago after we were married. There was supposed to be a lot of work for electricians because of the World's Fair coming up: "A Century of Progress." That sounded good to me. Next thing I knew he caught fifteen for armed robbery.

A friend of his took me on at the nightclub. He was the one that changed my name to Billie, said it went better with Frechette. He used to tell people I was French and Indian—"French where you want her to be French, and Indian where you want her to be Indian." I was used to the jokes. Before long I had me a Persian lamb coat and a long bob, and I'd learned how to cover smallpox scars with makeup.

Louis finally tracked Sparks down in Leavenworth and gave him Johnny's message. "What're you telling me for?" Sparks says. "We ain't married. I didn't even know she was using my name."

"Billie, Billie, Billie . . . you've lied to me so much," Louis says, "trying to keep me from finding this so-called husband of yours. Why did you give me all those names—George Welton, Welton Sparks, George Sparks? Why didn't you just tell me to look for George Welton Frechette, nicknamed Sparks? Why did you let me think Frechette was your maiden name?"

"All I'm asking you to do is check on his story before you say anything to Johnny."

"All right, tell me again where you were married."

"Chicago."

"Not Shawano?"

"We stood up in front of a preacher in Shawano, then when we got to Chicago, we went to city hall to make sure it was legal."

"So you were married in Wisconsin *and* Illinois."

"And one or the other's bound to have a record of it," I said, "if you just keep looking."

He always liked me, Louis did, but Johnny was the one he'd do anything for. He served time for the same rap as me—harboring a fugitive. I seen him just once after we both got out. He still looked like a kewpie doll with his big round eyes and round face. "I never told him, Billie," he said. "At least I spared him that." I couldn't figure out what he meant.

"He died not knowing that you could have married him *any time*. . . ." Tears actually rolled down his cheeks when he said it.

Mr. Dillinger always introduced me as Johnny's wife—at least until he got sore and stopped introducing me at all. "I first met the little lady *you're* waiting to meet," he'd say after his own talk, "back in April 1934. My son brought her to the farm. He had many women friends, so they tell me, but only two he ever brought to get his Dad's blessing.

"I warned him against the first one. I said, 'That girl will not stick by you,' which proved correct as he later admitted to me. But when he come leading this little lady by the hand—never mind state troopers watching the road, and G-men watching the house—I said, 'She's the one for you, Johnny,' and he said, 'Dad, I'm glad to hear that because I want you to meet the sweetest little wife in the world— Billie Frechette!'"

That was my cue to step out on the platform.

He knew from experience what people liked to hear, but I never doubted he believed every word he said, especially if it was something Johnny told him. He was supposed to have been strict in earlier

days. Wouldn't lift a finger to save Johnny from his first long stretch
—wouldn't pay for a lawyer—wouldn't even go to the trial. Prison
didn't change Johnny, except to make him a pro. The month he got
out he robbed ten banks in a row. It was Mr. Dillinger that caved in.
He used to tell audiences, "My boy lived longer in forty minutes than
I did in forty years"—something Johnny said once to a bunch of
reporters.

I never knew my own father—he was gone before I had the
chance. If I'd met him later, I wouldn't have cared two hoots in hell
what he thought about me. Johnny was just the opposite. I couldn't
get over the way he beamed when Mr. Dillinger took me around at a
family reunion introducing me as "Johnny's wife" and "my new
daughter-in-law." I was dying for a cigarette. "No—he don't believe
in women smoking!" Johnny whispered, nearly paralyzing my elbow
with his thumb and finger. His sister Audrey had to sneak me out
behind the barn. I was twenty-four years old!
There were relatives and friends from all around Mooresville at
that reunion. Naturally no one expected Johnny to show up—it
hadn't been six weeks since he busted out of Crown Point jail with
his "wooden gun," and the FBI had just promoted him to Public
Enemy No. 1. But when he got word from Audrey that there was
going to be a reunion, nothing could keep him away. "Fix yourself
up," he says. "I'm taking you to meet my dad."
We drove down from Chicago a day early, got there just before
dark. State police had the turnoff to the farm staked out, but he said
he had a secret way to get to the house that he'd used since he was a
kid. Nobody knew about it except him.
No wonder. We left the car on a back road, crawled through a
barbed wire fence, and started off through this maze of gullies and
ravines, some so deep I could see tree roots over my head. He was
carrying his Tommy, so I had to carry the overnight bag. I was
wearing a skirt flared at the bottom but tight around the hips, a
blouse with a lace collar, bolero jacket, and high-heeled shoes with
ankle straps. Fix myself up!

"The least you could've done was warn me to bring another pair of shoes," I said.

"Go barefoot."

The gullies were sandy but with a lot of little flat rocks. I remember thinking how tender my feet had got. Time was I could walk on cockleburrs and not feel a thing.

Mr. Dillinger nearly had a heart attack when he answered the back door, but right then, I'm sure, is when he took a liking to me. Not when Johnny got around to introducing me, but when he seen me following him barefoot.

State troopers and FBI cruised back and forth all the next day but didn't have no reason to come onto private property. There was just local people coming and going. Audrey and the others set up a big chicken dinner out back where Johnny could keep out of sight while everyone else let themselves be seen walking around and acting natural.

Afterward Johnny told everyone to gather around, he had a big surprise. He reached in his pocket and pulled out a wooden gun blacked with shoe polish. "Here it is, folks—the gun that locked up eight deputies and twelve trusties at Crown Point! Audrey," he says, "I'm turning this over to you. Don't you part with it for any price. Keep it and pass it on to your kids!"

For some reason Audrey flickered me a glance. I was hoping I didn't look more surprised than anybody else.

They all got out their Kodaks and begged him to pose with the gun. He said he'd do even better. He went in the house and got his Tommy. Mr. Dillinger stopped him on the porch. I don't know what he said but Johnny answered in a voice *everyone* could hear, "This Tommy's as harmless as that wooden gun. Sure I keep it loaded, but I never shoot except to throw a scare into someone that's trying to shoot *me*. That's one thing you don't have to worry about, Dad. I've never killed a man and I never will."

That night I asked him where he got the wooden gun. He gave me a hard look. "Why?"

"Well, you never showed it to *me.*"
"I made it in jail, just like I said."
"I don't think Audrey bought the story."
"Did she say anything to you?"
"No."
"Well, don't judge everyone by yourself."

Newspapers and public officals raised a terrible stink about that reunion. All those good people knowing the whereabouts of John Dillinger on that day, and not a one calling the law! He was still collecting newspaper clippings about himself. Only one thing bothered him—the way they kept referring to me as an "unidentified female companion."

"Now Dad will think I lied to him."

Mooresville people got their backs up at being called pro-crime. They sent a petition to the governor asking him to give Johnny a full pardon if he turned himself in. They said banks were as guilty as he was of taking people's money, only banks never got punished. They also said he wasn't violent, which was proved by the fact that he'd never killed a man. They wanted him to be given a chance to start over.

He was shook up by the petition. He said he'd written to some of the very same people at the time of his parole hearing, asking for letters of recommendation. "Not a fucking one answered! Now they see they were wrong—they want to make it up to me. They're good people."

I said, "I guess you're going to turn yourself in, huh?"

For a second I thought he was going to punch me—he couldn't stand not to be taken seriously. But all he done was say with kind of a sneer, "Why don't you wake up, Billie—broaden your horizons." A remark I haven't figured out to this day.

Once down in Florida he beat me up so bad Pete Pierpont had to drag him off me. That was Christmas Day 1933. Two black eyes, kicked my leg so hard I could barely walk, busted my lip. Red Hamilton, Boobie Clark, Chuck Makley, and Pete were downstairs, them and their girlfriends, having breakfast. It's funny Pete should be the only one to help me—his girl started the trouble, Mary Kinder. She was a tiny little thing but red-haired and mean. Johnny had gone down to the table and found his place wasn't set. In front of all the men, Mary said her and the other girls were tired of doing my work, said I never done my share, said she bet I was still putting on my makeup that very minute. Which happened to be true because of the smallpox scars.

I knew about how much good it'd do me to say that or anything else when he come slamming into the room yelling at me to get my ass downstairs and fix his breakfast! I said, "Well, what are you having?"

"Whatever the others are having!"

"Well, I hope it's bread and gravy, because if there are drippings I can make gravy, but that's all I know how to cook and I've told you that before."

"Then start learning!"—and he sends my makeup crashing to the floor.

I grabbed my long nail file. "I'm not starting *anything* just to please those bitches downstairs, and especially that one bitch!"

He swung on me, caught me in the mouth. Twisted my arm to make me drop the nail file. I went down on my knees to get it and he kicked me on the leg two or three times, hard. When I tried to stand up, I fell sideways on the bed. I went limp. I covered up my face with my arms and said, "Go ahead, show what a big man you are, prove you got power! The worst mistake of my life was to believe it myself!"

Then he begun accusing me of fooling around with someone else. That's what he always brought it down to. He never knew what I meant by power. "Tell me who it is or I'll kill you!"

So I said, "Charles Lindbergh."

He jumped on me like a mad dog, and I believe he would have killed me if Pete hadn't run in and stopped him. He was Johnny's best friend from prison, the only one he would ever listen to. Pete managed to get him out of the room into the hall. I didn't even care what they were saying, I was busy sopping blood from my lip with a wadded-up corner of the sheet.

Pretty soon Johnny come back alone. Didn't say a word. Grabbed me by the arm and made me sit up. Took my suitcase out of the closet and threw it on the bed, threw down a roll of bills. "Go back where you came from," he said, and walked out.

About an hour later I was limping down the stairs. Halfway down I heard Mary sing out, "Come on, everybody, let's open our presents!"

They were standing around the tree when I went by in the hall—taking their cue from Johnny and pretending not to notice me. Just as I got to the front door, Pete broke away. He said, "Wait on the porch. I'll call a taxi."

I said in a loud voice, "Don't bother, I got a car," and I jingled the keys to Johnny's new Ford. He'd left them lying on the bureau.

Pete stood there like he was frozen. After a couple of seconds Johnny said, "Let her have it."

So I went back where I came from—Neopit, not Chicago.

I could be gone a year and my mother wouldn't act no more surprised than if she'd seen me the day before. She'd always say she was expecting me because of a dream she'd had. I used to tease her. I'd say, "Oh, you're getting just like Grandmaw!" She thought she'd turned her back on the old ways, but she believed in dreams to the point where she didn't even say she *dreamed* this or that last night, but this or that *happened* last night. She looked down on the people over at Zoar, where they still lived in bark huts and belonged to the Medicine Lodge. She turned Catholic, she married a white man, she wanted overstuffed furniture, linoleum, and running water in the house, like the people over at Keshena. Still, there wasn't nothing she liked better than getting together with her cronies to swap tales about love powders and witches. On State 47, Neopit's right in between Zoar and Keshena.

When I drove into the yard she said, "I knew it was you. I seen your face in the water last night, so I knew you'd be crossing Wolf River today." I said, "Oh, you dreamed that because you want running water so bad." She pretended to think for a minute, then said dead-pan, "I believe you're right, Evelyn, and I seen your face because you're going to pay for it."

She was teasing me back. Other girls left the reservation and worked and come back with money to buy nice things. I usually showed up with nothing but the clothes on my back. This time, though, I had the Ford and the roll of bills.

I hadn't even counted it. She sat down and counted it first thing. Almost a grand.

"Well, it's all yours," I said. "Buy yourself a radio, get some furni-ture, have the front door fixed."

She acted uneasy. "I'll put it away and use it a little at a time." She wasn't worried about where it come from, only about being witched if someone got jealous.

A few days later snow begun to fall. "What are you going to do with that car?" she said.

"Leave it where it is, I guess."

Made no difference to me if it was buried in the snow. It got me where I was going, I didn't have no more use for it.

She went and borrowed a tarpaulin from a neighbor. *"You're* the one that's like Grandmaw," she said.

Mr. Dillinger used to tell people that Johnny was just an average American boy except for not having a mother after the age of three. He said Johnny liked to read Wild West stories, especially about Jesse James. He admired Jesse for fighting railroads and the money boys back East. Jesse was the one, he said, that inspired Johnny to respect women.

While he was giving his talk, he used to hold up baby clothes and a toy car he said was Johnny's favorite plaything and copies of Wild West magazine and family photographs in frames and souvenirs he said Johnny had sent him from different places, like a pillow with "A Century of Progress" painted on it. Then, at the end, with the crowd as quiet and respectful as church, he would unfold the suit he said Johnny was wearing the day he was shot. When he held it up you could hear people catch their breath because of all the bullet holes.

"That old man's a natural," Mr. Jax said. "Pay attention to what he does."

Because when I went out it was just like air leaking out of a balloon. Pretty soon I'd hear people muttering, "That ain't Billie Frechette." Crowds would get smaller after a few days, and by the end of the run there'd be hecklers. Mr. Dillinger could make people blubber, but it was me they were waiting to hear from.

Not long ago a woman reporter told me something about Johnny as a kid. The summer he turned thirteen he organized a gang bang for some of his pals. He didn't know any more about sex than they did—it was probably his first time. But he found the girl, gave a demonstration as best he could, then stood lookout while the others took their turn.

She asked if he'd ever mentioned this to me. I said no, but it didn't surprise me. I was wishing I'd known about it when me and Mr. Dillinger had our blowup. Just an average American boy!

Mr. Dillinger was plenty upset as it was. I said, "If you knew as much as you think you do, you'd know he lied to you about being married."

"You're the liar," he says.

"I was already married. And even if I *had* married him he would definitely have been second or third choice."

"Liar!"

I said, "You call me a liar again and I'm going to forget you're an old man and do something we'll both be sorry for!"

Mr. Jax had to step in between us.

Later he said, "Sometimes the Indian in you really comes out." I'd heard that before too. It could mean anything.

People didn't want to listen to another set talk after Mr. Dillinger got finished. They had to ask questions or bust. What was his favorite sport? What was his favorite song? Questions were tame back then. Usually they knew the answers better than I did. The first time someone wanted to know his favorite song, I said, "Home on the Range," and half a dozen people called out, "What about 'Happy Days Are

Here Again'?" "Well," I said, "can't a fella have more than one favorite?" I couldn't remember anything special about the way he
dressed. I don't think I *ever* knew what he liked to eat. Things like
that didn't make no impression on me.

Mr. Dillinger would get mad enough to have a stroke. "My son's
eyes was blue—not brownish-green or greenish-grey or any other
color except *blue!* He dressed in style, he had a ruby ring and a five-
hundred-dollar gold watch! Bread and gravy's what *you* like to eat,"
he said. "You're the one that likes 'Home on the Range' and baseball
games!"

"Is that true?" Mr. Jax said. "Is that what you've been doing?
Christ, Billie," he says, "it's only been two years. How could you
forget? Those were the days!"

Louis visited me right after I was sentenced. Johnny had just made
headlines again, shooting his way out of Little Bohemia Lodge. Six
people dead or wounded, something like that. President Roosevelt
went on radio to tell people not to glorify criminals. Everyone knew
who he meant. Louis said J. Edgar Hoover put him up to it because
Johnny kept making the FBI look like fools.

But Johnny was depressed, Louis said. "He's had enough, Billie, he
wants out. This time he means it. First he has to have plastic surgery.
While that's going on, I'll file your appeal. He wants you out in time to
go with him to Mexico."

"Don't do it," I said.

He wasn't listening. "Even if we lose, he'll be waiting for you when
you do get out. He said to tell you that. He said to tell you he'll do
whatever has to be done. You're the only woman he ever loved,
Billie."

He looked more like a kewpie doll than ever. I said, "Well, tell
him to take care of himself."

"Take care of himself! Is that the only message you have to
send?"

"It's a good message for him."

Which it was. Two months later he was lying dead in the alley by
the Biograph Theater.

One afternoon someone asked me how I felt about the Woman in Red—"him taking up with her and all that while you was in jail. . . ."

People had Anna Sage and Polly Hamilton mixed up then, or rolled into one. I wasn't clear about them myself. He walked out of the Biograph with two women, but one dropped out of sight so fast hardly anyone noticed her. Actually she was his new girlfriend—a call girl Anna had been using for bait. But it was Anna, wearing that red dress and fighting to collect the reward, that stuck in everyone's mind.

I said, "Well, I never expected him not to have another girl just because I was in jail, so I don't have no feelings about her one way or another. I never did have," I said.

Mr. Jax was waiting for me in the tent, shaking his head. We were getting near the Oklahoma line by then, "heading into real Dillinger country," Mr. Jax said. "We've got to get your act in shape."

I said, "Tell me what you want me to say and I'll say it."

"Next time someone asks about the Woman in Red, don't say you weren't *never* jealous, say in this case you didn't have no *reason* to be. Say you know from reliable sources that the Woman in Red was just a friend, someone that encouraged him to think of her as an older sister he could talk to and trust. She let him hide out in her place, then betrayed him—for money! Say you'd forgive him even if there was more to it than that: 'All of us have faced temptation and fallen. I will not cast the first stone. But I truly believe I have nothing to forgive him for. He was betrayed by a woman, yes! but not by the woman he loved!'"

"Well," I said deadpan, "if you want me to remember all that you'd better write it down. I'd never think of it by myself."

He lost his temper. "You claim you can't remember the color of his eyes, you claim you never got jealous! What the hell *do* you remember? What kind of feelings *did* you have?"

I don't know why everyone expected me to be jealous, like a witch. It was always the other way around. We hadn't been together two months before he took it in his head that I was making eyes at Eddie Shouse, a driver they sometimes used. Good-looking fellow, always had a girl on each arm and another one waiting in the car. I liked him but never paid no attention to his flirting. That's just the way he was.

But one day Johnny come storming in and pulled his .38 on me. "Get your hat and coat, you're going for a ride."

This was in Chicago. We were sharing an apartment with Pete and Mary. They heard him yelling at me, and come out into the hall in time to see him prodding me along with that .38. Pete says, "Use your common sense, Johnny. Shouse'll make a pass at anything in skirts. That ain't Billie's fault."

"She's leading him on. He wouldn't have the guts."

"What if she is?" Mary says. "She has a right to go for any guy she pleases. If she likes him, who are you to stop her?"

Which might sound like she was on my side, but really she was trying to stir him up more. It wasn't the first time.

He made me drive to a deserted stretch on the lakefront and park. "You got anything to say?"

"No."

"You don't seem to realize you're gonna *die,* sister!"

I didn't answer, just stared out the window on my side and thought about the wind blowing through the house, bare floors, bare walls, like sitting in the cockpit of a plane.

He said, "Remember what I told you when we met—that if you'd be on the level I'd give everybody the go-by for you?"

I said, "Well, I've been on the level. I can't help it if you don't believe me."

"I told you if you couldn't feel the same towards me as I felt towards you, then not to come when I sent for you—remember?"

"Yes."

"Why'd you come?" I couldn't think of any answer that wouldn't make things worse.

He said, "It's not enough for me if you just respect me, Billie. If you can't love me, I'd be better off not ever seeing you again."

I went on looking out the window. I wasn't going to beg.

"What's Ed Shouse got? What do you dames see in him? What makes you get all wet between the legs just because a guy's good-looking and has a fancy line?"

I turned and stared at him, disgusted.

He started rambling—all the women that'd let him down . . . his wife divorcing him while he was in the pen . . . a girl breaking off their engagement because she didn't want to settle down . . . another one skipping town with a square . . . he thought I was different, he was planning to take me to meet his Dad, etc., etc.

I thought, "Maybe he'll get it out of his system"—and sure enough, he trailed off after a while and lowered the gun and just set there. Then he all of a sudden grinned. "One thing I will say, kiddo, you don't lose your head easy."

I said, "Well, you ought to know that from just last week." I meant being with him in the Terraplane when he ditched four police cars—the wildest chase Chicago had ever seen. "I didn't lose my head because I know you're a good driver. You take chances, but I never yet seen you wreck a car."

"Put that in your purse till we get home," he says, handing me the .38.

He parked in front of the building and put his arm around my shoulder as we went up the walk. He rung the bell instead of using his key so Pete would have to look through the peephole. Pete really whooped: "They're back safe!"

"What happened?" Mary said. Johnny put on his best shit-kicking grin. "I couldn't do it. . . ."

I went on down the hall and into the bedroom. Mary followed me. I don't know what she had in mind, but before she could open her mouth I pulled the .38 out of my purse and pointed it right in her face. "Say one more word against me, bitch—ever—and there'll be some dead snatch around here!"

She backed out of the room, white as dough. She knew I wasn't kidding—and knew I wasn't just talking about Eddie Shouse neither.

She was at it again, though, in Florida. And twenty years later still at it. One July a Chicago newspaper run an "anniversary story" on Johnny's death, and reporters rustled her up for an interview. Not that it was ever hard to do. They asked if she knew what'd become of me. "Oh no," she said, "she dropped out of sight. Billie was a very unusual person," she said. "She didn't have a single good feature except her eyes. She didn't know how to dress or use makeup or do her hair. The rest of us couldn't understand what Johnny seen in her—except he was always for the underdog. . . ."

I asked him to stop teaming up with Pete. When the gang rented more than one hideout, him and Pete always went in together. I said, "I can't get along with her in the same *house,* much less the same *bedroom."*

"What are you talking about?" he said. "You and her don't do nothing."

"Well, neither do you and Pete, so what's the point?"

"The point is, he's my pal—and he likes company."

The questions the reporter asked made me realize how much times had changed. She looked like she hadn't been out of college more than a couple of years. Pretty too. But right away she wanted the dirt. "Was there any group sex in the gang?" I said I didn't think what we done could be called that—just sometimes we'd be in the same bedroom. "Was that Dillinger's idea?" I said it was the men's. "Did you detect any homosexual overtones?" No. "Did he force you to continue after you objected?" No.

And didn't force me to go to Tucson neither when he come after me all the way from Florida. *"That's* what people want to hear," Mr. Jax said. "Not how you wouldn't cook his goddamn breakfast!"

He drove into the yard and honked the horn. I looked out the door. "I'm here to repossess my car," he says.

"Well, it's right there in front of you, and the keys are in it."

"Who's gonna drive this one back to Chicago, that's what I want to know."

It was the first time he'd ever seen Neopit, and vice versa. My mother didn't have no idea who he was, even after I introduced him, but she said, "I knew somebody was coming. Last night Evelyn took the tarp off the car. I asked her what she was doing, I said it might snow. 'I know,' she said, 'but I feel restless.'"

He looked funny because the tarp hadn't been taken off the car, it was still there—but "restless" was just what he wanted to hear. He followed me into the kitchen. The first thing he saw was that picture of Lindbergh. "Nice-looking fella," he grins. Then started in on me to go with him to Arizona. The others were already on the way there from Florida. "I told 'em I had to go by way of Wisconsin. . . ."

"What's in Arizona?"

"A new life, Billie. I've got fifty thousand in cash. I've made my mark. Out there we'll be just a hop, skip, and jump from the border. After that . . . well, what do you say?"

It wasn't the money, it wasn't Mexico. I can't explain what flashed through my mind, but clear as daylight I saw that what was going to happen had already happened, and now I had to go through with it or it would always be waiting for me.

He'd dropped Red Hamilton off in Chicago. He went back to pick him up. They were supposed to meet me in three days in Aurora.

Instead he come by himself. We started driving day and night without stopping. I forget just where we picked up a paper with the headline, *Dillinger Wanted for Murder*. It turned out him and Red had robbed a bank in East Chicago but had been surprised by the police. In the shooting, Red was hurt; so was a cop. Now the cop had died. So it had finally come around. "That makes three of you," I said.

"Yeah, but they ain't got a case against *me.*"

No use reminding him that the only reason they had a case against Pete and Chuck was because they killed a sheriff springing *him* from Lima jail. He was too busy gloating over witnesses that were coming to his defense in East Chicago. "Listen to this: 'A woman who was cashing a check started to hand her money over to Dillinger but he refused it, saying politely that he was robbing a bank, not the people.' . . ."

All the papers played up how he turned back when Red was hit and helped him to the car. ("Hell yes," he says, "he was carrying the money!") "Four policemen had a clear shot at him during those moments when he refused to desert his accomplice, but as usual he was miraculously untouched in the hail of bullets. . . ."

Things like that sent him sky-high: "Miraculously untouched! That's me!"

What they couldn't do in Chicago, Indianapolis, or Minneapolis-St. Paul, they done in Tucson. Someone recognized Boobie Clark from a picture in the post office. The cops spent a day trailing us around, picking us off one or two at a time. No big gun battles, just a wipeout of the whole gang except Red Hamilton.

Three states wanted Johnny; Indiana finally got him. They took him to Crown Point because a new wing had just been added to the jail there, guaranteed escape-proof. To make sure, they put extra guards on duty around the clock.

The girls were packed off to Indianapolis—all except me. I suddenly found myself on the street, and Louis was handing me some money and a railroad ticket to St. Paul. "Rent an apartment and keep in touch. Johnny's orders." That's all he'd tell me.

The girls served thirty days. The fellows never made the street again. They were tried in Lima for killing that sheriff. Pete and Chuck got the chair. Boobie got life.

Johnny was charged with murder too. I went to St. Paul and sent the address. It wasn't over yet. I knew I'd see him again.

A month later he was knocking on the door.

There wasn't nothing miraculous about the escape. He had a real gun.

"Billie, Billie," Mr. Jax says, "how could anyone smuggle a real gun into the jail where *John Dillinger* was being held! It's against common sense."

"Well, how could anyone smuggle enough guns into Pendleton that Pete, Chuck, Boobie, and six others could bust out? But Johnny fixed it—the biggest break the state pen ever had. He fixed that, and Louis fixed this. Money," I said. *"That's* what's common sense."

He took two hostages and drove off in the sheriff's own car. He'd grabbed a machine gun by that time, but when he turned the two

men loose at the edge of town, he reached in his pocket and flashed a
.45 in front of their eyes. "Want to see what got me downstairs,
boys? Wood and shoe polish!"

They made the mistake of telling this to the newspapers. They
said they thought he was pulling their leg—it looked like a real .45 to
them. The tier guard that'd had it poked in his stomach said the
same thing. Nobody else got a good look at it. As soon as he got to
the ground floor and a machine gun, he put it in his pocket. Pretty
soon, though, everybody was talking about that wooden gun. It was
his story they believed.

In St. Paul, I asked him to show it to me. He said he'd left it with
Louis in Chicago—didn't want to lose it—someday it'd be valuable.
"I suppose you think it's a lot of hooey," he said.

"Well, seeing's believing."

I was joking and thought he was too, but all of a sudden he got
sore. "You'll see it," he says. "Don't judge everyone by yourself."

At the reunion Audrey slipped over to me. "I hope you don't mind
him giving this to me."

"Oh no."

She had a funny little smile. "Did you know I'm thirteen years
older than Johnny?"

"No. Why?"

"Oh, no reason. I'm the only mother he ever had," she said.

I told Mr. Jax I couldn't prove it, but in my opinion that wooden
gun was a cover story for Louis. Louis knew people thought Johnny
could do anything. If he said he rounded up eight deputies with a
wooden gun, you could forget about anyone suspecting a fix.

Mr. Jax got as sore as Johnny. "That gun's part of American
history! But if it *was* a cover story—which I don't believe—then it's
to his credit that he didn't tell you."

No use saying that wasn't the reason.

I said, "Know who else he didn't tell? Pete and Chuck. They tried
the same thing on Death Row, using soap intead of wood. Chuck
was shot to pieces, and Pete burned right on schedule."

He said, "Billie, if you want people to like and respect you, you better get over trying to debunk John Dillinger. That's not what you're getting paid for," he said.

Funny, but the night before that reporter was due I was sitting at the kitchen table and all at once I could remember letter-perfect everything Mr. Jax and Mr. Dillinger ever wanted me to say. I thought, "Well, better late than never." I needed an operation for a little growth on my neck—I was hoping she'd help me out, me giving her an exclusive interview and all. I was ready to start with how it was love at first sight when Johnny walked in the nightclub, and go on from there.

She was polite but she set me straight in the first ten minutes. "Billie," she said, "I'm not here to get the same old Robin Hood line. The angle I'm working on is the truth behind the macho legend."

He had a gun in St. Paul I hadn't seen before. It wasn't wood, though—it was a pistol-sized machine gun that he could hide under his coat. He'd had it made special. He tried it out on jobs in Iowa and South Dakota while they were still looking for him in Chicago, and he used it when they finally caught up with us early one morning in St. Paul. He fired through the door, driving them back, then tore the hall to pieces while I flew down the back stairs wearing nothing but my slip and Persian lamb. I backed the car out of the garage, but he wouldn't get in—he kept shooting up the rear end of the building. "For God's sake, get in!" I screamed. He didn't care who he killed.

He was bleeding in one leg, so I had to drive. How we got to Minneapolis I'll never know. All I can remember is what a relief it was to see daylight again. In St. Paul we had to keep the shades drawn, couldn't go out till after dark, had to sneak down the back stairs. I never did get used to hiding out.

He was stretched out on the back seat. I heard him mumble, "You're okay, kid."

"Thanks."

"Yeah—you too," he says after a second.
I looked around. He'd been talking to that gun.

This reporter had her own ideas about guns. She brought up Clyde Barrow, George Kelly, Baby Face Nelson. The only one I knew was Baby Face. Kelly's wife, though, was on my tier in Milan. She had it in for me until she saw I wouldn't pull rank on her. I never talked about Johnny at all; she talked about George all the time—mostly trying to convince us that she'd been the real brains of the Kelly gang, and if he'd listened to her, they'd be out "drinking good beer," as she used to say, instead of doing life. She liked to read his letters from Alcatraz out loud and make fun of the mushy parts. She said she didn't know how he ever got the name "Machine Gun" Kelly—people might *think* he could write his name on the wall with bullets, but he couldn't even *hit* a wall. Her name was Kathryn.

I was picked up not long after Nelson joined the new gang, so I didn't know him very well—though as well as I wanted to. A mean killer. It was worth your life to call him Baby Face. As far as I could tell, his wife was crazy about him.

Johnny took him in after Crown Point, along with some others of the same kind. The only one left from the old gang was Red. On the Iowa and South Dakota jobs he shot out windows, kicked hostages, cursed at women, and went out of his way to kill. "I don't like it no better than you do," Johnny says to Red, "but that's the way they want it." By "they" he meant the cops, the FBI, the banks. The same line he peddled at the reunion.

Red wasn't fooled. "Johnny won't have to worry about his rep," he said to me on the sly, "as long as he's got Baby Face."

It was Baby Face the public got down on. Once when they were using two cars, someone threw tacks under his tires but not Johnny's. He died in a ditch. The body wasn't even claimed.

Johnny was laid out in state in the morgue. Lines a quarter of a mile long. Someone selling pieces of cloth they said had been dipped in the blood in the alley. Mr. Dillinger went to get the body. Lines outside the funeral parlor in Mooresville. Big mob at the cemetery. Couldn't hardly get the coffin out of the hearse. Tombstone chipped to bits as quick as it was put up. Mr. Dillinger said he had to have the casket dug up and set in concrete, then concrete slabs poured in the dirt over it. "People wouldn't believe he was dead, they wanted to see with their own eyes."

You couldn't feel sorry for him—he was too pleased and proud. "Audrey chased two fellers back to their car one day and seen California license plates!"

From Minneapolis we went to Chicago, then to the reunion, then to Indianapolis, then back to Chicago. I could almost feel the wind at my back. We shouldn't have gone near Chicago—the heat was on worse than anyplace. But he was in an ugly mood, he wanted to see Louis in person. "I'll give him one more chance. And then—" He cocked his finger at his temple. He was hell-bent on making good that lie about us being married.

Louis tried to get out of meeting him; he was sure he'd be followed. But Johnny wouldn't take no for an answer and wouldn't explain what he wanted on the phone. Finally Louis agreed to meet him in a bar on North State Street about ten p.m.

I knew he'd spill the beans if I didn't get to him first, so when Johnny was parking the car I said, "Let me go in ahead of you to see if the coast is clear."

He looked at me kind of funny—I didn't usually volunteer—and besides that, the Feds now wanted me for harboring. Then he said, "Okay, but if he ain't there, *scram!* Don't hang around."

The place was crowded—I couldn't see him—but I hung around for a few minutes in case he was in the men's or something. I heard a car horn blasting away—I don't know why it didn't register sooner. I beat it for the door—I could hear a motor being gunned—tires squealing. I run right into the big paws of the FBI.

"What's the matter?" I said to Mr. Jax. "Does it sound like I'm blaming him for making his getaway? Tell me what you want me to say. It wasn't his fault; I done it to myself."

He wouldn't answer, just looked at me.

"Well, not on *purpose,*" I said, "if that's what you're thinking."

We hit a spell of cyclone weather down near the corner of Missouri, Arkansas, and Oklahoma. Twisters like rattlesnakes all through that section. We'd be coming to a town and see a rooftop hanging in a tree, or a telephone pole sticking through the side of a barn like a toothpick. Everybody's nerves were on edge.

One afternoon—I remember how sultry and still it was—a woman asked me how many scars Johnny had on his body. I'd never been asked that before, maybe it seemed too personal; but whether it was that or the weather or what, I went blank. I said, "Well, he had a scar from climbing a barbed wire fence as a boy. . . ."

There was some shuffling around, people cutting their eyes at each other. "She means from the times he was shot," a man said.

"Well, he was pretty lucky, you know. He got creased a lot of times but he didn't really have what you'd call scars—no, not that I remember."

"She ain't Billie Frechette. . . ."

Mr. Dillinger had been laying off me for a while—now he landed with both feet. "My son was hunted and hounded and cut down in cold blood, and you tell people he didn't have no scars! I was the one identified the body, I *seen*—" He broke clear down.

"Well, I didn't say *no* scars, just none I could remember."

"If you can't remember, who can?" Mr. Jax said.

All of a sudden I screamed, "Anybody'd think I spent my whole life with John Dillinger instead of one piss-ant year!"

Mr. Dillinger turned and walked out. "I won't be on the same platform with her no more."

Mr. Jax didn't run after him. He knew who was leaving and who was staying. "Billie, Billie, Billie . . . you're just not making 'em believe that you were the love of his life."

"Or vice versa."

He wasn't interested in that, never had been. "I'm gonna have to let you go, Billie."

He was right about one thing—the Woman in Red took my place. When I left the carnival, I pledged not to talk about John Dillinger again. Every now and then someone would track me down, but I stuck to my rule for thirty years.

I didn't mention money until this reporter was in the house. "I've had to scramble these past few years. Take a look around," I said, wishing I hadn't had my hair touched up—her eyes went right to it.

She was interested in what I told her about Kathryn Kelly. "Mightn't she have been saying he wasn't so hot in bed—'couldn't hit a wall' with his gun?"

"She was disappointed in him, but *brains* was what he didn't have."

She asked if Johnny had anything to "compensate for." "Was he underendowed, for instance?"

"That'd have to be in his opinion, wouldn't it?"

"Not necessarily. *Was* it his opinion?"

I said I didn't know.

"What about Harry Pierpont?"

"Pete? How would I know? Ask Mary Kinder."

"She's been saying for a number of years that they weren't lovers, more like brother and sister."

"Well, that's news to me."

"Did you ever sense that Johnny was showing off for Pete—to help him along?" I thought: If any of this is true, no wonder Mary Kinder hated me!

I wasn't surprised when she begun to lose patience with me. I could read her mind a mile off—I was one of those women that men make doormats out of. Half Indian besides—probably didn't care much about sex, just laid there. My opinion of her was she had a one-track mind.

"Listen," I said, "I'd like to help you, I could use some money, but as far as I'm concerned you're barking up the wrong tree."

She asked what I thought her angle should be. I couldn't explain. I kept wanting to say, "Well, he was deceitful in the way the old people say evil spirits are. He didn't really have a shape of his own, he could only *take* shapes." I thought, "The older I get, the more I go blanket, just like Maw. . . ."

When I was in the hospital with my neck, I found a book by Lindbergh's wife on the bookcart—diaries and letters telling how they met and such. I felt sad seeing pictures of him looking the way he looked on my wall. He had a smile that lifted right off the page, the clearest eyes. I remember when I first tacked his picture up. I was seventeen. My mother said, "Who's that?" Without even thinking I said, "Someone that's got Power."

"What do you know about Power?"

She never had told me about it, of course, but I must have picked it up somewhere. "I don't know if it's the same," I said, "but if a white man can have it, he's got it. I can tell by the eyes."

His wife saw it too. Oh, she fell hard when she met him. She told herself she wasn't going to be taken in, but something burned like a bright fire in his eyes. He made her feel like he could do anything. The minute he proposed she said yes. She didn't expect it, didn't want the kind of life he was offering, but what could she do? There he was, she said—she had to go.

My mother studied that picture several days before she said anything. Then all of a sudden she started talking about the old ways. "When I was a girl, I went out in the woods and fasted so that I would see the future. Back then young girls who seen the sun or wind believed they'd find happiness, they'd get a good husband. But in my dream the wind was pressing like a hand against my back, pushing me faster and faster along a road until I was almost skimming. I turned my head and seen a tall dark shape, but I couldn't make out any feature except his eyes—cold and blue as ice, but at the same time they burned. I told my mother and she said I'd seen the Wandering Man, a spirit who never rests but goes round and round the earth with a burden on his back. He takes many different shapes, but when you see him, it means misfortune unless you perform special ceremonies."

"Did you perform them?"

"I started to, but I quit because I was in school; I was afraid to ask the Sisters for time off."

"About payment—" this woman said.

"Forget it," I said, to save her the trouble. "I never could make anything out of John Dillinger."

The Upper and the Lower Millstone

The king of Jericho lived in a state of rising hysteria. His soldiers combed the streets looking for spies, and arrested people for throwing rubbish over the wall—though this had been done for so many years that the dry moat was filled and the rampart half-covered before anyone ever heard of the people of Israel. Instead of having the rampart cleared, or the wall repaired where it was cracked and eroded, he ordered the earthquake intervals filled—as if they were flaws!—so that there was no longer any way to isolate collapses—the whole wall would fall down flat!

The other kings of Canaan shunned treaties of mutual defense with him—they seemed to regard the fall of Jericho as inevitable, perhaps unimportant. Deadliest of all, rumors circulated that the Egyptian garrison would soon be withdrawn, Pharoah having succumbed to the view that his real interests lay further north.

Blind! Deaf! Were the rumors true? The captain of the garrison would say neither yea or nay, but took refuge in maddening Egyptian non-answers—"All would be as Pharaoh wished. . . ." The king stamped his feet, ground his teeth, and behaved ever more irrationally, as on the day when he summoned Rahab to a private audience and demanded information from *her*.

"What information could I have that you have not?" she cried indignantly.

"You—the captain's harlot—what information!"

"I've heard the rumors everyone has heard, nothing more."

"Your protector hasn't set a date, then? Hasn't said goodbye?"

"No."

"Then there's still time for you to prevent it."

"I? Pharaoh moves the garrison, not I!"

"But you move the captain. Your witchcraft is well known. Re-double it. Bind him so fast he'll persuade Pharaoh that remaining here is a military necessity—as it is," he raged, "though I won't try to explain that to you—much less appeal to a nonexistent loyalty. For you I have just this one word of warning: Jericho's fate is your fate. If Egypt pulls out, don't imagine that you'll be going along. If their terror—" he pointed east across the Jordan—"falls on Jericho, you'll be here to suffer it. Beware! They have a god fiercer than Reshef or Mekel—he made the waters stand up on either side and crash down like a wall on Pharaoh's horsemen and chariots. What they did to Heshbon in the land of the Amorites you know. Never again will the Amorites boast in song, 'Fire went forth from Hesh-bon, flame from the city of Sihon.' Furthermore, mistress harlot, they abominate the flesh—there are none of your profession among their women. So be moved—be moved by practical considerations, if not by the plight of Mother Jericho!"

Rahab went home with an angry smile. Mother Jericho! From a brigand who collected taxes two years in advance! And, while the Hebrews were swarming up from the south like locusts, razed houses and shops to make room for more royal stables, larger palace gar-dens! Nor was she pleased at being called harlot. In that, as in his demand that she serve Jericho, she heard the groan of a long-suppressed passion. When he first set eyes on her, she already be-longed to the captain. Was that her fault? Where in *any* of this was she to blame? What justice in threatening her?

Nevertheless, she made special preparations for the captain's visit that evening. Because the king's passion had never been satisfied, he could not conceive that the captain's might be dulled—that he might be more friend than lover these days, likelier in fact to go apart with one of her little sisters than with her. But so it was. Witchcraft in-deed would be needed to make things otherwise. She hung an amulet of Astarte around her neck, one of Asherah around her

waist, bound another of Anath to her arm. Whether they were one
goddess or three she had never known. She prayed to the first while
she scented her body, to the second as she painted her eyes, to the
last as she thickened her hair with dyed rope. Then she poured a
single libation to all-in-one.

The captain came bringing a gift—an amethyst ring set in gold.
Exquisite. It should have been a good omen, but was it? "They don't
make things like this anymore," she murmured. She didn't mean
that he'd probably gotten it from a grave robber but that he could
hardly have gotten it anywhere else in these times of cheap ivory
plaques and fake scarabs set in copper.

He followed her thought with his customary Egyptian ease. "On
the other hand, where but in Jericho could one find these extraordinary tables?"

She smiled—with a chill in her heart. Jericho's furniture was a
long-standing joke between them—he pretending to be unable to get
used to tables with two legs at one end and only one at the other, she
exclaiming (as she did now): "Why, surely wherever the ground is
uneven they have such tables?"

"Practical Jericho!" he said. "I assure you that in other places
they stupidly level their floors."

"I wonder that Pharaoh can abandon us when we have so much to
offer. Why does Egypt prove faithless?"

He studied her with his long eyes. "I know about your audience
with the king."

She flung herself at his feet. "I wouldn't stop you if I could! I
don't care where you're going, or when, or why—only take me with
you!"

"You shouldn't let tales of the Red Sea frighten you."

"It's not the Hebrews I want to flee, but this dunghill Jericho!"

"The same story will soon be trotted out again," he said, just as if
she hadn't spoken. "When they come to the Jordan they'll turn up-
stream—to Adamah perhaps, or some other place where they can
tumble a cliff into the river and dam it for a while. Then they'll cross
dryshod and swear their god parted the waters. They produce these
miracles especially for Canaanites. Pharaoh isn't moved by signs

and wonders but by practical considerations. Jericho is no longer vital to his interests. The trade route to Syria is."

"Speak more plainly. Will you take me with you?"

"What about your family—your father and mother—the sisters?"

"What about them?" she asked, startled.

"Suppose the king sends after you and I refuse to give you up? He'll take revenge on them."

"He won't send after me, he won't do anything! Your informants took his rantings too seriously."

He saw things differently. "The moment a departure date is announced he'll issue a decree: no one from Jericho to accompany us in our 'flight'—not a saddlemaker, not a baker, not a wife or child. He'll dress up this childish spite as pride—'Mother Jericho'—but he'll be in deadly earnest. You, my Rahab, would become a traitor, not "—he again surveyed her with his long eyes— "a loving mistress."

"I'll hide in a basket—among the provisions—you needn't even know where!"

"And your family?"

"Bastard! Son of a hippopotamus! When have I ever shown this family feeling you're suddenly hiding behind? My loyalty for seven years has been to you—to Pharaoh. Am I not called 'the Egyptian woman'? Take me with you!"

Even as she raved and pleaded she knew she was wasting her breath. There was goodbye in the amethyst ring—in the familiar joke—in the disparagement of the Hebrews—but most of all in the appeal to practicality, that thing which those having the upper hand called down like a curse on everyone else. What she proposed was not "practical." Pharaoh wanted him to leave with as little incident as possible. She wanted to involve him in an act of rebellion. He advised her to be patient. Seven years, after all, though muting desire, had not left him entirely without a sense of obligation. He would find some less provocative way to achieve what they both wanted. . . .

And so he passed out of her life, or withdrew from it. When the king's soldiers found her—in a hamper of raisins slung on one side of an ass—he didn't even turn back from the head of the column to investigate the commotion.

She was not, to be sure, the only deserter rooted out that day. But whereas the others were strangled and thrown over the wall, she was offered a way out, and did not scruple to take it. Yet she fell on evil days, for there was so much muttering against the king's mercy that he scarcely had time to enjoy it before he was forced to withdraw it. Torn between Baal-tyranny and Anath-lust—or rather, twisting in the single grip of the brother-sister, king-and-consort pair—he spared her life, saying privately that the criticism would soon die down, while blustering publicly that disgrace would serve justice better than death. He denied any other motive for letting her live, and to enforce belief turned her out of the house the captain had given her, seized all her movables except some jewelry, and drove her back where she came from—back down among the rout and rabble who lived against the wall. At the same time he privately ordered her to reenter the house of her parents, where he would set a secret guard to keep her safe until he could again put his left hand under her head and embrace her body with his right. Until then (he half-groaned, half-snarled) he would sleep with a waking heart; and she—she must keep herself as a garden that is enclosed, or a spring shut up, or a fountain sealed. . . .

Rahab's heart burned in her breast. Seven years earlier, with the light of Astarte just beginning to gleam in her eyes, she had stood in the door of her father's wineshop and turned the captain round-about in his tracks. But who was the more dazzled? Egypt seemed to promise an escape from the anarchy of Jericho. She gave herself willingly, not because it pleased and profited her father. She was proud to be called the Egyptian woman. Yet what *was* Egypt finally? Repository of strength, order, beauty? Yes, as the grave is! Truly the Land of the Dead—her people empty vessels, her promises a scroll that is rolled up! Strange and bitter that Rahab—who, above all women, craved, above all things, principle and consistency—should find only caprice and disorder wherever she looked. Chaos had returned, as it always did in Jericho. Now she must go backward in time and place, must—ultimate anarchy!—be born again to her father and mother.

They wailed and beat their hands together over their heads. What had she ever done for them in these seven years, except take her sisters off their hands? Now even that was undone! Her mother climbed the ladder to their house on the wall and would not come down. She had borne two sons in Rahab's absence. The younger, still in swaddling clothes, she kept as well hidden as if he were not. There was talk these days of reviving the old custom of infant sacrifice to the War God, and she was filled with dread that Rahab would bring this fate upon him. The father, blind with cataracts, crouched in the door of the shop and implored passersby not to ruin him because of his daughter's transgressions. He could hear hissing in the streets, and vows—made or extorted—never to cross the Egyptian whore's threshold.

Notwithstanding, her disgrace was short lived. Besides the fact that the wineshop was near the East Gate, where traders and farmers came and went, there was that exceeding beauty, not to be hid among jars and bushels in the storeroom over the shop. Like that of the Mistress-Virgin (who bore the lily in one hand, the serpent in the other) it fascinated and disarmed. Business revived—improved —needed only to be put on its true basis to flourish as never before.

To that end Rahab looped her braid forward, like the tail of a scorpion ready to strike, and paid her mother a visit. "The little sisters and I are no longer content to sleep on mats in the storeroom," she said, gazing all about but letting her eyes rest especially on the lolling, misshapen head of her younger brother. He had been conceived too near the upper limit of childbearing; he would never—even if such a danger existed—make a suitable offering to the War God. His mother, however, gathered him up as if he were some precious possession and, muttering charms and scattering signs, moved into the storeroom that very day. Rahab and the sisters took possession of the house on the wall.

This was no more than a one-room mud-brick hut—there were several near the East Gate, where the oldest and thickest part of the wall stood. Some were larger than anything below—in places the wall was thirteen feet thick; and most had windows with refreshing outward views. Rahab could look down on emerald fields near the city, a stretch of pale desert beyond, and in the distance the Jordan flowing among dark-green tamarisk groves. But houses were not built on the wall because of any such advantages. Actually they were extruded by the crowding below. The advantages were accidental and revocable. A window looking out of the city meant a house set between the king and his enemies. Any dwelling below was preferable. Now, however, Rahab saw an advantage she hadn't seen before; and she proceeded to make use of it.

The wineshop and storeroom were connected by a ladder that rose from the street, but the house on the wall had its own ladder at the end of a short alley alongside the shop. Patrons inflamed by wine and Rahab's beauty could be sent discreetly outside, around the corner, up to the sisters—who sat waiting, each in her own newly curtained-off alcove. Not that either sister was treated like one of the women who crouched by the side of the road, wrapped in the veil of a harlot—both had Rahab for their sign and shrouding garment, and she was discriminating on their behalf. Some patrons grumbled because she herself did no consorting. Most felt, mysteriously, that she did not and yet did; and that they had possessed her even when they not not, as goers-in to temple prostitutes might feel both embraced and not embraced by the Goddess.

She prospered, and could expect to prosper more as harvest time approached—but, like someone in exile, uncertain of deliverance, she was restless and dissatisfied. For a time she vented her feelings on her father: "What! Fallen silent? No more whining at the door? You bleated like a goat when I tried to save myself by leaving Jericho. Now that I'm abandoned—and all your daughters whores!—you smack your lips and count feet crossing the threshold. This is a father indeed! Pimp! Jackal!"—and so on, until he would gladly have joined his wife in the storeroom had not the clink of coins and shuffle of feet somewhat drawn the sting from her contempt.

Then she fell to mocking Jericho; and though this was especially ill advised now that the people of Israel were rumored to be hastening toward Shittim, just across the Jordan, still she compulsively paraded the little store of knowledge she had acquired from the captain. If someone said thankfully that the Jordan was beginning to overflow its banks as it always did at harvest time, she would say that the god of the Hebrews made a specialty of heaping up waters. But if someone babbled fearfully about the Red Sea, she would say that no miracles would be needed at the Jordan—only common sense on one side and negligence on the other. The Hebrews had no battering rams? No weapons except curved swords and old-fashioned square shields? No chariots? Well, but they had legs, hadn't they, to carry them up ramparts littered with footholds? Arms to hurl torches over the wall onto thatched roofs and wooden beams? The wineshop buzzed at her audacity. Did she know more about these things than the king? Undoubtedly he had some plan to prevent the wall from being turned into a fiery furnace. "Oh, undoubtedly," she would reply with a fine smile. "After all, he has only to look down from the palace to see what the problem is."

The king's men, knowing his obsession, had been reluctant to accuse Rahab of harlotry—especially when, in a technical sense, they might be wrong. They were doubly quick therefore to report signs of her other disloyalty. They did not, of course, accuse her of directly aiding Jericho's enemies (though she had commanded a room with a window on the Jordan and was not scrupulous about giving a warning to outsiders when the city gates were about to close for the night). But at the very least she was encouraging defeatism and panic.

The king went for her in secret; no sooner saw her again than he began to writhe in the double grip.

"Why do you prolong your exile?"

"How do *I* prolong it?"

"By drawing attention to yourself—arousing suspicion."

"Of what?"

"Of . . . unfaithfulness to the king," he said ambiguously.

She had come prepared to defend herself against a charge of harlotry and said promptly, "I am no harlot but an honest inn-keeper."

"No harlot?" he echoed.

She saw that she had made a mistake and, as if it had been deliberate, asked mournfully: "What else could I be accused of that would so distress my lord?"

He gazed into her eyes, deep as the deep spring that had drawn men to Jericho time out of mind: "Take care, Rahab! I would lead thee and bring thee out of exile—let there be no spot in thee! Take care whom you speak to with your lovely mouth—whom you see with those eyes like doves' eyes—what you say with those lips like a scarlet thread. Oh thou absolutely fair! I would bring thee and lead thee— my left hand here—my right hand there—and yet I do not love thee absolutely—beware!"

He refused to be—perhaps could not be—more coherent. Next day, however, soldiers came to block up her window, and she noticed that a political informant had taken the place of one of her guards. She felt no fear, only disgust. While the Hebrews licked up the land across the Jordan the way an ox licks up grass, the king of Jericho took measures—against Rahab! Not for harlotry, which would have made some sense, but for hand-me-down criticism!

She waited three days, then knocked the bricks out of the window. The sisters were appalled and refused to obey her any longer. They crowded into the storeroom with the mother—who unaccountably made them welcome. Rahab shrugged. She would replace them with daughters bought from poor farmers. Meanwhile she put the room to a use which had tempted her before. She began to harbor outsiders who had no permits to stay in the city overnight. Since the penalty for this was high, so was her price. Then she ceased to be, even technically, a garden that is enclosed, or a fountain sealed. If an after-dark supplicant could pay the price she asked for the room, he could very likely pay an added sum as well. Seldom, at any rate, did a lodger refuse to empty his purse when Rahab came gliding through the curtain—wily as a serpent, yes, but beautiful as a garden of lilies glimmering in the dark.

Because it went somewhat against her grain to enter upon the sisters' work, she trafficked only with these profitable few. She seldom took in more than one; some nights, none. If a search party broke in, she could claim she had been lied to. Or perhaps not. Her defiance had reached fever pitch and cried out to be heard.

As it was; for now the Hebrews appeared on the opposite bank of the Jordan. They had arrived speedily at Shittim and encamped there. Advance parties were already scouting fords and river crossings, as if no amount of flooding would stop them. Panic spread through the countryside. Farmers deserted their fields and tried to move inside the walls. The king drove them back, saying that fruits and grains must be gotten into silos, sheep and cattle into pens. Typically he didn't look to prices. Uncontrolled, they shot up uncontrollably, with the result that only palace and patrician granaries were filled—public ones remained empty. Sheep and cattle clogged the narrow streets on their way to the palace and to patrician dwellings, where ground-floor rooms were being converted into pens. The turmoil at the East Gate each dawn and dusk threatened to overwhelm the guards. To importunate farmers were added refugees from across the Jordan and all manner of other unidentifiable outsiders. Permits to enter the city or to remain were ignored, evaded, falsified, gotten by bribery, theft, even murder. Dwellers inside the wall began to clamor for the gates to be shut up. The king replied that the harvest was not half in. They pleaded for more haste in filling public silos, lest the Hebrews prevent it altogether. He sent word that the Jordan would detain the Hebrews—the real enemy was within; and he multiplied the patrols which scoured streets, shops, and houses. When cries arose that these were not efficient but only capricious and brutal, he multiplied them again.

Rahab's personal overseers disappeared. The wineshop was harassed like any other—or rather, more than any other, in line with its reputation as a meeting-place for conspirators. Business was not affected. A raid might empty the place for a while, but customers soon jammed in again. People were not opposing the king; they had simply ceased to support him. They were waiting for a miracle, and whether it saved or destroyed them seemed not to matter. A kind of madness for oblivion had seized them—even if the sisters had not retired, they would have wanted only wine, more wine.

Rahab rarely went down. The passivity and defeatism repelled her. Even her own rebellion was faltering. Though she now stood ready to hide lawbreakers who could pay little or nothing, suddenly there were fewer coming to her door. Paradoxically, these few never lacked money. Several times search parties invaded the house—but only by day. She might have seen the signs but didn't. She supposed it was only a matter of time before a patrol would burst in after dark. In this she was correct. One night she was arrested, next morning taken before the king. Their meeting was not private this time but well attended by courtiers and soldiers. She did not expect to return from it. In that, she was wrong.

He began a little distance away from the arrest—with the daytime search parties. "You are accused of saying that your window was unsealed by my personal order."

"Yes."

"In case the room should be needed for military purposes."

"A plausible lie. Was it believed? I told it more than once."

"So plausible it will soon become truth." He looked around the court for approbation and got it, but misunderstood Rahab's expression—she was shrinking from the thought that she might be forced to move in with her mother and sisters. "Not that you'll be compelled to practice your profession by the side of the road," he said. "At least not right away. Until I need the house for my purposes, my soldiers will use it for theirs."

She spat.

The king smiled and combed his beard with his fingers. "You scorn my soldiers? Look around. Don't you see even one you've already entertained? You there, take off your helmet—plead for an overnight hiding place. Do it in a low voice."

Rahab saw with disgust that the grinning soldier was the man she'd been arrested with.

"I see you do recognize him. There have been others, too."

"Yes—and still others *not* sent by you!"

"No doubt. It's reported, though, that you never ask your visitors any questions."

She was silent.

"Except about money, of course." He looked around with a broad smile. "Well, that was wise, Rahab. For if you'd asked these men how they happened to get trapped by the shutting of the gates— whether it was by accident or design—and if you'd hidden only the ones who answered 'By design,' then I would have to charge you with treason. But it appears that your house—and your person—have been open to anyone, not reserved exclusively for the enemies of Jericho. So it was only whoredom after all. Some few may have been spies and saboteurs, but how many more weren't even violating the curfew! I don't mean the ones sent by me, but those others you boast of. Did you expect your generosity not to attract men who would swear falsely that they were fugitives?"

"I wouldn't expect anything else in Jericho."

"Oh, Jericho—Jericho knows the difference between rebellion and harlotry. It is Rahab who dresses up one as the other."

Rahab, swaying like a lily on its stalk or a serpent on its tail, raked the court with terrible eyes: "I'm glad these the king's dependents have had so reassuring a demonstration of the king's good government. He has proved Rahab a whore! Can anyone then doubt that he'll prove a bulwark against Israel? Ah, what Heshbon could have done with such a king!—the Amorites who will never again boast in song, 'Fire went forth from Heshbon, flame from the city of Sihon.'"

The king did not look around for fear of seeing only downcast eyes. The mockery that he alone understood angered him more than the rebuke that everyone understood. But it was exactly his purpose to discredit damaging notions about their intimacy, and he did not allow his condescending manner to be shaken:

"Rahab has already shown that government, like gratitude, is beyond her comprehension. She does so again. A careful king concerns himself with everything that might affect the welfare of his subjects. Though his vigilance consume and exhaust him, he cannot prejudge whether a matter will be great or small. Luckily, this of Rahab proved small, unimportant—mere whoredom, as I have said. I would have been remiss not to look into the other possibility, but now I say in justice: Go home, Rahab. You are free to resume your trade—bound only to practice it honestly. It will be the only livelihood open to you, but the one you know best. If you're tempted to play any other role, you must find a better way to unmask those who will be role-playing with *you*. My advice is, stay in your own depth. You will not suffer by being honestly what you are. My soldiers will see to it that your house becomes as well known by day as it was by night. However, you can hardly succeed if you go back to fobbing your sisters off onto those who thirst for *you*. It is my express wish that you and you alone—"

Long before he finished (the court egging him on, as if in these convolutions they saw a proof of strength) Rahab had stopped listening. She scarcely heard the jeers that followed her out of the palace. At the wall she saw without seeing that the wineshop had been boarded up. Her father came to the foot of her ladder, wailing and clutching the air. She did not answer but stood at her window, staring eastward. It might be, as the captain said, that the Hebrews prevailed not by miracles but by foresight, planning, discipline—yet she was ready to believe now, as the wineshop did, that they also had some Power which went before them and prepared the way. Until today she had wanted Jericho to remedy its follies, at worst had only wanted to leave it. Now she craved to see it lying in the dust—a heap of ruins forever!

Late in the afternoon she heard the sisters sniffling at the door. She faced them venomously. "Well?"

"The wineshop—closed—the king's orders—"

"Well?"

They fell to their knees and knocked their heads on the floor, weeping. "The father said you wanted to see us."

She felt a twinge of pity mixed with irritation. "I bought some flax, simpletons—I need you to help me carry it to the roof."

They looked mistrustful but hastened to lug the bundles through the trap door. She did not help them. A moment or two later she went up. "So—I must do it all alone," she said with a crafty smile. "You don't want to help me. . . ."

They began to weep again. 'It is not our fault—"

"What is not?"

"We are afraid—"

"Afraid—to spread flax out to dry?" They rolled their eyes at her. "What did you think I meant? Untie the bundles!"

She noticed the trembling of their fingers—felt another twinge of pity—then, suddenly, anger so overwhelming that she fell to screaming like one possessed: "You cannot do even this thing right! The stalks must be laid in order—tops this way, roots that way—not scattered about like straw and dung! In rows and ranks—thick here, thin there—else how shall we ever turn and dry them evenly? Cannot even such sluts as you comprehend rot? Oh thou befuddled—unteachable—malicious!"

She seized a thick stalk and began beating them. She could see herself, hear herself; but, as if she were divided, she seemed to be shouting something that set the walls to swaying. The sisters teetered on the brink of the trap door—she saw them drop from sight as the walls collapsed outward, slowly, as in a dream, and so compactly that they girdled Jericho with a broad pathway leading to destruction, and every man came straight ahead of him into the city—

"Greetings to Rahab!"

Her outer vision cleared. Two young men stood in the alley below—one already had his foot on the ladder. She moved back from the edge of the roof. Out in the street a party of soldiers grinned at her, gestured obscenely, then moved on through the gathering crowd toward the gate. In either direction the wall stretched away intact.

The young men were waiting nervously outside her door. She seated herself on a mat and spread her skirts out all around her; she was perspiring, disheveled; bits of flax clung to her skin and garments. They stared doubtfully when they came in. "Rahab the innkeeper?"

"Rahab the harlot!" she said with harsh emphasis. "But the soldiers mocked you. They know well that the custom of women is upon me. I am unclean."

They seemed to bow a little. "Our Rachel," they murmured. "So said she when Laban pursued Jacob. Hide us from our pursuers, as Rachel hid the teraphim from hers!"

"Ah—you are pursued! Why? The gates are still open. If you came in without a pass, you can surely go out the same way—"

"Our life for yours!" they interrupted fiercely.

"Do you intend to murder me? Very well, but don't plan to stay here afterward. This is the first place the king will look—if indeed he *is* looking and hasn't sent you to entrap me."

"The king is hunting us—now! His men are watching for us at the gate—now!"

Her inner vision began to confuse her again. She fought to stay clear headed. "Why? Who are you?"

"Deal faithfully and kindly with us now and we will deal kindly and faithfully with you when the Lord God delivers the city into our hands!"

The walls fell outward with a rush and roar, paving and preparing the way. Amid the din she had one clear thought: the soldiers hadn't *sent* these visitors, but they *had* seen them. Time was short. She couldn't wait till dark. She must hide them now.

She went up into the deceptive twilight and resumed spreading the flax. At her signal they wriggled through the trapdoor and onto the roof, as flat on their bellies as snakes. When she touched them with one hand, they ceased and lay motionless. She began to cover them with flax she held in the other hand.

"I know your god has given you the land," she whispered in their ears. "Fear of you has fallen upon us; we have heard that you prevail not by miracles but by planning, discipline, cooperation for the common good—"

They rustled under the flax like adders trod upon. "Have you not heard how the Lord dried up the Red Sea when we came out of Egypt? and how—"

"Yes, yes," she said hastily. "I only meant that no such wonders will be needed here. Your report will show it: the condition of the walls, the faintheartedness of the people. This business of yours will prepare the way. . . ."

They were covered to their chins, visible only in profile; for a moment she did not understand the smiles they exchanged. "So be it. Do not tell this business of ours and we will spare not only you but also your father and mother, brothers and sisters. Them too we will save alive."

"Them too?" she echoed inadvertently. Then understood: they thought she was bargaining! This was not some of the captain's trickery—they expected it, approved of it.

"We have sworn. . . ."

"Well, I will keep my part," she said, and covered their faces.

Just as she expected, the king's men arrived before the closing of the gate. She had changed into a soft white robe that left one shoulder dazzlingly bare, and was braiding her hair with scarlet yarn when they burst in.

"True, two men were here," she shrugged, "but who they were or where they came from, I don't know. I'm no traitor but an honest harlot, as the king commanded. Two men, that's all. True, they delayed until a short time ago, then jumped up and ran, as if they'd suddenly remembered the gate would close at dark. If they did leave the city, they can't have gotten far. Go after them now and you can overtake them. Or," she said indifferently, "if you don't believe me, you may use your time searching the house. . . ."

When total darkness fell, she called the men down. "As soon as your pursuers rode out, the gate was shut. They'll be back when they can't find you. There'll be no hiding place in the city, and especially not here."

"You have heard what we did to the kings of the Amorites," they began, "to Sihon and Og—"

She was searching through a chest for a rope, and cut them off impatiently. "Go into the hills behind the city—hide there. They'll be watching the fords of the river."

"With respect to the oath you made us swear," they said as they secured and tested the rope, "we will be guiltless. Gather your family into the house when we come before the walls. If anyone goes into the street, we cannot be responsible. But all who stay in will be delivered from death."

She wasn't bargaining—the rope was already dangling out the window—but: "This house? When the city is under siege? Give me some token—some sure sign."

They turned to gaze at her admiringly. "Our wise Rachel! That scarlet cord—bind it in the window on that day."

"This?" she said incredulously.

"The Lord will pass through to smite the Egyptians but when He sees the blood on the lintel and side posts, He will pass over the door and will not suffer the Destroyer to enter and smite you. . . ."

Words dark as the darkness at the bottom of the rope. She was disappointed at their riddling way of speaking, as if plainness were not enough. Nevertheless, she coiled the rope and laid it in the chest,

coiled the scarlet yarn and laid it inside the rope. Against the day.
Words aside, she had seen the fate of Jericho.

Now the city was strictly shut up. None went out and none came
in—expect Rumor with her thousand tongues: the Hebrews had
crossed the Jordan and had not; had come through dry-shod or half-
drowned; were turning back at Gilgal or regrouping there. People
heard sappers at work under the wall—felt quakes and
tremors—saw pillars of fire in the shape of a drawn sword, or raised
trumpet, or uplifted arm. One morning the entire city suffered what
seemed to be a mass delusion. Out of the desert came a great host of
armed men, perhaps forty thousand in all, moving in perfect silence
and order. Half preceded a band of nine priests; half came after.
Two of the priests bore a golden chest slung from poles; seven carried trumpets made of rams' horns. As the advance host reached the
corner of the city, the seven raised their trumpets and shattered the
very air. Roundabout the city the eerie procession marched, and still
the forty thousand uttered no sound, but the trumpets blew con-
tinuously. One circuit only—then gone again into the desert.

On the second day they did the same, and every day thereafter for
six days—by which time they were no longer delusion but waking
nightmare. At the first blast of the harsh, unceasing trumpets
people went into convulsions, beat their foreheads on the ground,
stormed the gate crying for release into the hills. Afterward they
wandered up and down the streets with vacant eyes and twitching
mouths. The king withdrew into silence and seclusion, as if a spell
had been woven round him. His commanders fought for pre-
eminence. Soldiers received contradictory orders and manned the
wall haphazardly, their morale melted away.

Rahab's house was forgotten. She stayed in it undisturbed.
During the first march around the city she went down to the storeroom to gather up her family. If the Hebrews valued filial piety, she
would display it! But her father and mother rebuffed her soundly,
even reproached her for unseemly exultation. "Stay here then, and
be slaughtered with the rest!"

She was not inclined to see black magic in the silent marching and brazen trumpets. She admired the controlled and channeled energy, but as she might admire it in a troupe of acrobats; she awaited the issue. By the sixth day nonetheless she felt a kind of panic. Suppose she alone were saved? She alone taken to dwell among strangers? Her father and mother, after all, had never mistreated her out of ill will, only out of poverty and fear—and she and the sisters had been close. . . . She hung the scarlet yarn out her window and hastened down to the storeroom.

The sisters were lying in a corner with pillows over their heads. The brothers were squalling horridly. "Today is surely the day!" she said wildly. "There is no time to explain or beg! Destruction is at hand!"

The father and mother shook their heads, but their refusal was not so categorical this time. They seemed, in fact, ashamed. The sisters sprang to their feet. Without waiting for permission, they fled. "Leave us," murmured her mother. "See, your sisters have gone—return after them. . . ."

"Entreat me not to leave you! Where I go, you will go, and where I lodge, you will lodge. Today our lives will be delivered from death. Afterward, where you die, there too will I be buried!"

She found herself shouting in a sudden overpowering silence. The incessant blare of the trumpets had stopped. Her father put out his hand—whether to find hers or to steady himself was all one. In that moment the house shuddered profoundly—a wooden box pitched out of its niche in the wall, scattering the sisters' little supply of combs and shoulder pins—the older brother sat down flat, his legs stiff with surprise—a row of wine jars skittered out of line. *"Now!"* said Rahab, seizing her father's hand. Just where he would have touched the wall, a crack opened up from floor to ceiling.

"No!" her mother said sharply. "Your brothers!"

Rahab obeyed; carried one, dragged the other through the stampeding crowd. The attackers had broken their silence; the air throbbed with their high-pitched ululating battle cry; it seemed to pierce and dissolve the very bricks and mortar that would keep them out. At the top of her ladder Rahab handed the boys to the sisters, then turned to look for her parents. They were just struggling into the alley, the mother leading the father by the hand—urgently but carefully, so that they would not be torn apart in the chaos. . . .

Touching, yes—but oh, to have been at the window or on the roof, instead of waiting at the door! By the time she gathered her parents in, the wall had been breached, the Hebrews were in the city. They were scrupulous about their oath—and prompt. The East Gate, out-flanked and under attack from within, was quickly abandoned. Almost at once two men—the same two men—came to hurry the family down the long ramp leading from the Gate to the plain. As they set their faces toward Gilgal, they were sternly warned not to look back, lest they be turned into pillars of salt. Rahab supposed this meant to become transfixed by tears, and did not hesitate to disobey, though surreptitiously. Armed men were still scrambling up the littered rampart, but not every man could go straight ahead into the city. The ways were few and narrow, some had to be bloodily forced. She could see one place only where the wall had fallen out-ward as in her vision, one section carrying another down with it. Other gaps were isolated, as if the earthquake intervals had done their work in spite of the king's tampering. Stretches of the wall that remained standing, however, were being fired with brushwood debris. The very bricks turned red, and bursts of smoke and flame rose on the other side.

By nightfall Jericho was no more. Word raced to Gilgal of the solemn curse Joshua had laid on any man who should ever try to rebuild it. "A heap of ruins forever!" exulted Rahab. She only regretted that she hadn't seen every step in that great downfall.

For a while she was a heroine. Joshua summoned her in order to look upon her and thank her for saving his spies. Marriages were arranged for the sisters—they accounted for their lost maidenhood, little hypocrites, by way of husbands who had refused to flee the wrath to come. The father and mother were treated as blessed among parents, a role they played with laughable seriousness. Rahab, at least, had to smile when she heard them praise her for her modesty, her piety, her many devoted services—a daughter if ever there was one!

No doubt they sensed that she would soon become a problem. Nothing, unfortunately, could prevent it. She could not remain unmarried when every man who saw her lusted for her in his heart. But who among the married men would risk domestic upheaval by taking her as a second or third wife? Or who among the young men would want her for his first? Even at the height of her popularity she was secretly called "the Canaanite *zonah*"—a word that might mean "innkeeper" only but also "keeper of a house" in a worse sense. Who would give his mother such a daughter-in-law?

Rahab helped in her own swift fall from grace. She was disappointed to find idolatry flourishing in dark corners—images, charms, potions, spells for warding off or curing sickness, divining the future, resolving matters of the heart. In the last she might have earned gratitude, since women were inclined to regard her as possessing both natural and supernatural powers in love. But when they came to her secretly, she rebuked them, saying they were no better than Canaanites; she marveled at their disrespect for their own Law, not to mention their lack of fear of Joshua. Had they not seen the same thing she had seen after the sacking of Jericho? The man named Achan had hidden a bar of gold and two hundred shekels of silver under his tent, instead of putting them in the common treasury. Joshua made every tribe pass before him; chose one and made every family in it pass by; chose one family; then one household; then finally, infallibly, confronted the hidden faithless individual.

Rahab had been impressed equally by his intuition and by the swift, incorruptible justice that followed. "As for me," she said passionately, "I would strive rather to be worthy of such a man than go about to deceive him!"

Nor did she approve of the version of the fall of Jericho that began to take shape when the women sat in a circle clapping their hands and making up verses. For a while she held her peace, then not: "I saw! I was there!" Joshua had cunningly demoralized the city—devised stratagems to nullify a river and wall—taken quick advantage of an unexpected stroke of luck. They disparaged him when they substituted mere wonders for hard work and foresight: heaped-up waters! walls struck flat! an angel taking charge the night before!

Ah, if the people of Israel could live just one day under the leadership of the king of Jericho!

"More Israelite than the Israelites!" they said behind her back.

They also detected something they thought was more in line with her real character than a desire for righteousness. Joshua was a handsome, vigorous man in his middle years. He was not, however, married—a condition the women had never regarded as anything but temporary, celibacy being as inconceivable to them as profligacy was abhorrent. The mere possibility that Rahab would breach that wall—the great probability that she would try—the utter certainty that she would like to—sealed their antagonism toward her.

She might have told them that, from the moment she met Joshua, she knew he was wed only to his mission. She had seen celibates before. He called her "my child" and was remote as a monument. She would have been disappointed to find him any other way. But their spitefulness so angered her that she deliberately put out a flickering tongue, musing aloud upon that other leader whom everyone seemed to value so much more highly than Joshua. Moses had married an Ethiopian, had he not? And when the woman Miriam spoke against it, behold, she was made leprous, white as snow. Was this not true?

"We are weary of our lives because of the Canaanite *zonah!*" the women said to their husbands. "If he marries such a woman, why should we go on living?"

The men had been away at the siege of Ai and the rout of five kings at Gibeon. They were not surprised to hear that Rahab often thought of Joshua, and ordinarily would not have been alarmed if he sometimes thought of her. But there was an element in their wives' complaints that went beyond female envy, something touching their very enterprise. Soon they too were saying, "If he is beguiled by a woman such as this, what good will *our* lives be?" The question was how to set the matter before him with the proper emphasis. They had no wish to be misunderstood. However else he fell short of Moses, it was not in wrath and denunciation.

While they debated, Joshua looked around and saw for himself that Rahab was shunned. It seemed ominous that she was troubling Israel just when he was preparing to move against Lachish, Libnah, and cities of the south, to do to them what he had done to Jericho.

He demanded that his advisers tell him what she had done, and to hide nothing from him. Then he sent for her.

She had been expecting a summons and took care to answer it with unenhanced beauty. But though she suppressed her lily side, when she stood before him in the presence of witnesses she succumbed to the other and gave an angry, twisting reply: "I've done nothing, said nothing except to give credit where it is due. You must ask those who complain of it why Joshua makes them weary of their lives, or arouses evil imaginings—why they whore after magic and miracles—why they set Moses' heel on Joshua's neck—"

He cut her off with a gesture, set aside his remote manner, and said with terrible directness: "Why will you be a stumbling block to me, beguiling me with words and tempting me to vaingloriousness? Why will you be a thorn in the side of the people? Soon all Israel moves south to lay hold on the Promise. What meaning will their lives have if their victories glorify *me?* One man of them puts to flight a thousand because the Lord God fights for them. They keep me from pride when they say, 'There has not arisen again in Israel a leader like Moses, who saw the Lord face to face, none like him for signs and wonders, and for great and terrible deeds.' They do not exalt me further than I exalt them, for I also remind them and say to them, 'You are mighty men of valor because you obey the Lord.'

"The night before Jericho," he said, after a pause in which he resumed his cloaked and withdrawn air, "behold, a man appeared to me with a drawn sword in his hand. I said, 'Are you for us or against us?' He said, 'I have come as commander of the army of the Lord.' I fell on my face and worshipped: 'What does my lord bid his servant do?' For He alone had the whole circumference of the wall in view, to strike it flat or leave it standing, in whole or in part, all at once or in good time. What He did, He did. Give glory and thanks to Him, as those to whom you slander by saying, 'I saw, I was there.' All who were there saw through a chink. They are not the ones who whore after magic and abominations, but you—who credit Joshua with deeds no man could do, the Lord not commanding!"

Rahab bowed herself to the ground. It was a moment when she could have wished the walls of Jericho would rise again. Between that tyranny and this demagoguery, what was there to choose? Like a grain of wheat fallen between two millstones, she waited to be ground up.

The silence, profound as that silence when the trumpets ceased to blow, was broken by a voice she did not recognize: "The woman has behaved foolishly out of ignorance, being a foreigner. She deserves this rebuke, but now remember what she did for Israel, under whose wing she took refuge. Remember also, Joshua, that Moses was called 'very mild, more than any man on the face of the earth.'"

Rahab did not dare look up. And indeed, almost before she herself could find out who had spoken, the whole camp knew that it was the honored young man Salomon. He had turned Joshua's wrath aside, so that she was not cut off from Israel, nor even put outside the camp for seven days like Miriam, but only told to go and make ritual atonement of the easy kind allowed to foreigners, and afterward to dwell in peace in Israel.

Even if this mildness had displeased the people, there would have been no arguing with Joshua. Salomon stood too high in his esteem. He had just returned from Shechem with the good news that the king there was friendly to Israel and would allow a cadre of officers and advisers to be planted in his city. Joshua, planning to lay hold first on the cities of the south, then the north, needed an ally betwixt and between; he had dispatched Salomon to get one for him soon after the crossing of the Jordan. The victories at Jericho, Ai, and Gibeon helped persuade Shechem, of course, but no one—least of all Joshua—underestimated the influence of Salomon's agreeable manners and worldly temperament. He was just such a man as could make the Promise seem desirable and not merely inevitable.

The people were not displeased with his intervention on Rahab's behalf. They seemed, rather, to be greatly entertained by it.

> *She tied a red string to Joshua's hand,*
> *But Salomon made the breach!*

they sang, muddling the facts a little but getting at the truth. A few days after her atonement Rahab went to draw water, and Salomon, in sight of everyone, followed her to the well.

She tried to be gracious but was sore at heart. Her atonement had been a form and a lie. She thanked him for judging her kindly and made a move to leave. When he begged her to stay she said somberly, "Look around you—all Israel is watching—they're laughing at you with their hands over their mouths."

"I see them," he said easily. "I even know what they're saying: 'The tribe of Judah—naturally!' or 'What else?' I don't mind. Anyway it's the truth. We *are* self-willed, passion-prone. A scarlet thread runs through all our history."

"Is that why you take notice of me—a foreigner?"

"Exactly my point," he said with a smile that acknowledged *her* point. "Perhaps you've heard of Tamar?"

"No."

"She was a foreigner too."

"Then she was to be pitied."

"Not at all. She triumphed exceedingly."

"I should like exceedingly to hear about her—sometime."

He was not easily put off. He told her the story then and there, resting his arm on her water jar so that she could not lift it to her shoulder and be gone. He had a way of speaking that surprised her—both serious and self-mocking. She hadn't heard the like since Jericho. It should have refreshed her; instead, it made her uneasy. And the tale! The woman Tamar, twice widowed and childless, wrapped herself in the veil of a harlot and enticed her father-in-law to lie with her. When she conceived and was brought up on charge of harlotry, she produced certain tokens he had given her and forced him to acknowledge his part. Was there ever a sorrier, more confused history? It seemed to Rahab to defame the Canaanite woman and make Judah her victim. Where was her triumph, except in low trickery?

"Why, in justice," Salomon said good naturedly. "Judah himself admitted that she was more righteous than he. She'd been married to his first two sons. When they died, she was entitled by law to marry the third. Judah promised but procrastinated. He was fearful for his third son's life—though Tamar had nothing to do with the death of the other two; they were struck down from their own wickedness. Why should she, a young woman, be cut off and remain a childless widow all her days?"

"But she conceived by the father, not the son—"

"He was the one who'd reneged."

"—and played the harlot to do it!"

"Truly—'played.' Judah, though, was *not* playing. His sin was like scarlet. Of course," Salomon added, "he atoned."

"And his tribe has many such tales?" Rahab asked in a neutral tone.

"Oh, many! Perhaps you've heard of Pharez and Zarah? No? Well, when the time of Tamar's delivery came, there were twins in her womb. During labor one of them put out a hand, and the midwife tied a red string to it to show that he'd arrived first. But suddenly the hand was pulled back—maybe voluntarily, maybe not. His brother came out instead. The midwife named him Pharez—Breach—because, she said, 'I tied a red cord to the other one's hand but this one made the breach.' Pharez was the founder of my clan."

"So I supposed," Rahab murmured.

"Sitting in the door of Joshua's tent on the second day of my return," he said in his half-eloquent, half-humorous way, "I raised my eyes and saw a young woman pass by with a water jar on her shoulder. Whether she was foreign or a daughter of Israel I couldn't tell—only that my soul fainted within me. I was saying something about Shechem to Joshua—the thread snapped, like that! I demanded to know who she was—and learned that this was Rahab, whom I alone had not set eyes upon."

"And when he told you that this same Rahab was making Israel weary of its life?"

"My soul fainted a second time—from jealousy! 'She praises Joshua?' I said, or stammered. 'Why should that offend Israel?' Then he told me he had sent for you—I could hear and judge for myself."

"So that was the way of it," she said, half to herself. "You weren't there by accident. . . ."

"How could I be?"

She stared at him with eyes that no longer saw him. She was again in Joshua's tent—bowed down in profound silence—hearing the eloquent plea—and Joshua's abrupt response—one following the other so closely they might have been twins. "You judged kindly—you turned away his wrath," she said, but it was more of a question.

"Did I? Well, if you like . . . though really he only sent for you to remind you that no man is good, none righteous. A useful thing to remember, especially in leaders and governors."

"So that was it!" she burst out. "I suspected it! He denounced *me* in order to flatter *them!*"

"Don't you think it cost him something to refuse that flattering worship of yours?"

"No, nothing—he gained by it."

"Or I did," Salomon said gracefully.

"It wasn't worship," she brooded. "It was admiration for a mortal man."

"You're still free to admire him."

"Luckily I'm forbidden to praise him. I'd be at a loss unless I should praise his adroitness in demagoguery."

"Joshua—a demagogue? You're too categorical."

"What is a man who denies vainglory in one breath and receives angels in the next?"

"Well, these are less heroic times than formerly," Salomon said with an enigmatic smile. "The Jordan isn't the Red Sea. The conquest of Canaan won't rank with bringing the Commandments down from the mountain. That's the burden he bears. Still—he has to lead. Must he proceed entirely by rule, law, statute, ordinance, covenant? Can we do entirely without inspiration? At least he's clear on the point that he doesn't talk to the Lord face to face, as Moses did. . . ."

She knew he meant to put a hand under her foot when she was in danger of sinking, but the comfort was less than it should have been and did not increase in the days that followed, when he came to her father's tent. He reminded her obscurely of the captain. He was partly soldier but mostly diplomat, emissary, negotiator; therefore somewhat lacking in sense of outrage. He expected flaws and failures—they were embedded in some larger scheme of things which required patience to unfold. Any other attitude, he said, was impractical.

The captain! To have come all this way, only to find herself back at the beginning!

There was, however, this difference: When Salomon departed for Shechem with the cadre, she was not left behind. She went with him as his wife. Or was that only a seeming difference? Once again she was helpless to oppose what was happening to her. Salomon passionately desired it. Joshua, with an air of dignified relief, gave it his blessing. Her father literally died of joy: sealed the contract, then fell on his back, staring upward as if blinded by a miracle. The sisters, now more Israelite than the Israelites, were, like Joshua, content to see her go, but they must remain with their husbands. They pressed the mother to stay too, but she elected to hold Rahab to a former promise. Shechem, she had reason to believe, was not unlike Jericho, for which she increasingly had secret fits of nostalgia. "'Where you die, there will I be buried'—you have said it."

"Yes," answered Rahab. "I have said much in my time."

She'd been given one vision of the future but was not vouchsafed another. She joined her nature to Salomon's willy-nilly, so to speak, and bore him a son named Boaz—the same who comforted Ruth when she was a stranger in the land. His son's name was Obed; his, Jesse; Jesse's, David; and so on in that half-practical, half-passionate direction. In time Jericho rose again. People went back and rebuilt it, not knowing or not caring that Joshua had cursed it "forever." The spring there was deep, the waters living. The story does not record, however, that any of Rahab's line ever looked back. It is not there that she dwells "to this day."

The Education
of Michael Wigglesworth

Who Later Wrote the Great & Useful Poem
"Day of Doom"
& Became America's First
Best-Selling Author
Anno 1662

In the spring of 1646 George Spencer, a laborer, was brought to trial in New Haven for bestiality. The sin was hidden but the fruit made it known. A sow belonging to Goodman Wakeman gave birth to a monstrosity: a piglet with one eye only in its forehead, and that over-hung with a loose flap or growth—pink, fleshy, hairless—resembling nothing so much as the male organ of generation.

Goodman Wakeman called to his wife, but only to say that the sow had littered and that one was not normal. Goody Wakeman came to look, turned pale, and fell a-murmuring to herself. He asked her what she saw. Nay, she asked, what did *he* see? The thing of flesh, he answered, that was like a man's. Aye, she said, so it was! But let him look also upon the eye—whitened over, blind, somewhat distorted, but also like a man's. And so it was! he said.

They buried the prodigy in worried silence, but not their misgivings. The uncanny would not down. What think ye?—nay, what think *ye?*—until at last Goody Wakeman blurted it out: the eye resembled George Spencer's, who sometimes worked for them. He was dimwitted and had a pearl in one eye but was otherwise strong and serviceable. Several others had also hired him, including Goodman Wigglesworth. But if God chose this way to point an accusing finger at him, dared they say, We will not look where He points? And so George Spencer was arrested upon their complaint.

Provokingly he swung back and forth between blubbering confessions in prison and indignant retractions in Court. He would say that his private confessions were meant to please his questioners the magistrates, but that these worthies had no right to ask him to repeat the same things in public. The things were not true! Only ingratiating! Why would they not understand?

The Reverend Mr. Davenport was called in. He visited the prisoner in company with six magistrates, one being Mr. Cheever the schoolmaster. George fell to his knees at once and confessed everything. But this time his visitors did not leave, uttering comfortable words. Mr. Davenport would have none of it. He remained fixed in his place and pressed for details. How long had George Spencer been under this temptation? Had he sought religious counsel? When had the act taken place? Where? One time, or more? How was it accomplished? With what thoughts, what feelings?

Thus Mr. Davenport rubbed raw the guilt that was in danger of scabbing over, forcing the sinner to live the shameful time over again: the troubling unnatural lust—the neglect of wholesome counsel—the sow lured and driven into a barn—forequarters pinned and roped between two slats—hindquarters gripped so—then the maneuvering this way and that—until his will was accomplished, accomplished. . . .

He ended his tale face down in the straw of the prison floor, groveling at Mr. Davenport's feet. He seemed almost changed into a swine. The other worthies drew back, appalled. Not so Mr. Davenport, who knew what to expect of human nature. He leaned down and said to George Spencer that he had turned this room into a pigsty before their very eyes—he had done the thing over and let them witness it! And would he dare come into Court tomorrow and claim he had performed such filthiness to please them? Or would he say that any was gratified save only himself?

George cried out that he would never again deny his great guiltiness. He begged Mr. Cheever to stay with him so that he would not cheat the Court by killing himself! Which Mr. Cheever did. Yet, on the morrow, George again recanted.

The Court, put out of patience, condemned him to death anyway. The law was intended to make justice perfect, not to forestall it. If (they said) George had been advised by someone to stand upon the letter and not the spirit of the law, he had been most wickedly advised.

On the gallows, slobbering and beshitting himself, George rolled his good eye piteously about and spied Will Harding in the crowd. Suddenly he began to bellow: There was the man! Will Harding the sawyer, who had visited him in prison and told him he would not hang if he kept retracting! Because of Will Harding he had angered minister and magistrates—brought law and religion into disrepute—brought himself to the gallows—when he might have truly repented and perhaps saved himself! Will Harding should be in this place, not George Spencer!

The Court hanged him, then turned its own eye upon Will Harding. He admitted visiting George in prison—the poor fellow had no friends or family—but as for acting as attorney, he was at a loss to account for such an accusation, except that it came from a frightened and muddle-headed creature. . . . The Court drew down its mouth. Men did not lie on the threshold of eternity, not even weak-brained ones. However, since proof was lacking, Will must be let go. The Court admonished him—and settled back to wait. Sooner or later, being what he was, he would deliver himself up.

For the saints were not alone in New England; they did not have Canaan to themselves. Swarming across the Atlantic in their wake came a whole host and crew of laborers, artisans, craftsmen, apprentices, domestics—some indentured, some free, but all called "servants" because they did not share in divisions of land but performed services for others. They professed to have the same goals as planters, but experience indicated otherwise. In Mr. Davenport's view they were more likely being sent to test the whole great experiment of setting New England on a hill to be a light to the world. Unfixed, unchurched, intractable in morals (but quarrelsome about rights), they formed a churning demoniac underside that continually challenged downward-seeping righteousness with upward-thrusting corruption.

Mr. Davenport often brooded upon this ill company in his sermons, and was moved to do so again after George Spencer was hanged. On successive Sabbaths he dilated upon the laborer worthy of his hire, as it says in Luke 9:13, and then upon those caterpillars of the commonwealth who crept in under the guise of good and faithful servants. Though not planters and often not church members, they were given the use of a piece of land, sometimes a house, sometimes a sum for supplies and equipment. They had no vote but were allowed to speak in town meetings. They were protected by the Court in their persons and property.

Their gratitude for these favors was to be little in performance but much in disturbance. The worst was not excessive wages, shoddy workmanship, sale of unlawful goods to the Indians, sleeping on watch, breaking the Sabbath—though these offenses and more abounded. The worst was the insinuation of themselves into the fellowship of the young people of the town. In this they had an almost intolerable advantage, for (Mr. Davenport said unflinchingly) children of even the godliest parents were bent and biased by fallen nature toward wickedness and frivolity, and needed but little encouragement to resist reason and religion. Year by year, he mourned, those lights who first led the way into New England were dying off, diminishing in number. If the second generation failed to follow this goodly company, if they were enticed by ill company instead, would not New England be left in utter darkness? Then indeed might fathers and mothers, teachers, magistrates, and other guardians of the young cry out, Woe unto us for our spirit of toleration!

Among Mr. Davenport's hearers none was more affected by such warnings than Edward Wigglesworth. His conscience had never ceased to trouble him since the time, four years earlier, when he had withdrawn his son from school and cast him (perforce) into the company of hirelings.

Mr. Cheever was accustomed to such withdrawals in the spring and fall, when boys were needed for plowing and planting, reaping and harvesting. But it was also common for a boy who had learned to cipher, write a little, and read in Scripture to be called out and kept forever—even so forward a one as Michael. Therefore, said Mr. Cheever, he felt duty bound to call upon Goodman Wigglesworth to sound out his intentions. Was Michael to be taken out of school permanently? New England could not thrive without learned men, especially in the pulpit. In Massachusetts a college had already been founded to receive and train new lights. So far New Haven alone had been unable to spare a single one of her sons. And now Michael, of all Mr. Cheever's young Samuels the most promising, he too was wanted—for plowing!

Edward said bluntly that he could no longer spare his only son's labor. He had no indentured servants as yet and must rely upon hired ones, who were both overpriced and in short supply. Such felling, cutting, piling, and burning; such plowing, harrowing, delving, dunging, sowing, and reaping; such hewing, hammering, bending, joining, lifting, and lowering as one man could do, he had done. He did not complain of the sweating labor (which God had ordained for man), but only of falling behind others in the number of acres he brought under cultivation. When he saw what return there was, from but little seed, of wheat, corn, peas, beans, barley, rye—indeed, of all fruits and grains; when he saw New Haven's newly completed Long Wharf stretching out into the harbor like a funnel through which foodstuffs would pour to New Amsterdam, Virginia, Jamaica, Barbados, to Nova Scotia, Portugal, Spain, the Canaries, the Azores, nay, to England herself!—when he saw all this his conscience smote him for neglecting his son's practical education. Michael was ten years old, yet except for the care of animals, for which he had shown some aptitude, he had little knowledge and no skill in husbandry. But God had not led the children of Israel out of Egypt so that they would remain in their Egyptian condition, rooting about like Indians and laying no hold on the Promise. If Edward was ever to bind laborers to his service (as in time he would), and if Michael were not to work alongside them and remain a goodman all his life too, then he must learn to manage and oversee fields, men, cattle. . . .

Mr. Cheever now saw what he had not seen before and had not expected from this quarter. He drew his brows together and asked which the father preferred: to have his son called "Master Wigglesworth" because he owned lands and cattle, or because he had Learning?

Edward said he meant only that here in New England both ways were open, whereas in Old England, Michael could never, unless by a fortunate marriage, have become a freeholder of any consequence, though he could have become a minister—

Yet he left off this way of answering, for Mr. Cheever's wrathful countenance made him uncomfortable, and so did his own conscience. If Michael really were another Samuel for learning, dared his father curtail his education, cut him off from offices requiring learning—especially the ministry? He was puzzled by his own lukewarmness, but since he was not in the habit of heeding motions in himself which he could not account for, back to school went the young Samuel.

Less than a year later he was out again. This time Edward could not prevent it, and indeed could not well avoid seeing God's will in it, since he himself was made to suffer to bring it about. Which might have seemed unaccountable except that God, infinitely wise and absolutely sovereign, had not to account for any of His proceedings. If it pleased Him to visit Edward with lameness and by that means settle the problem of Michael's future, then so it was and so it would be.

One cold day, while Michael sat in Mr. Cheever's parlor, warmed by a sufficient fire and his teacher's attention, Edward was working on a desolate section of burned-off land with an ox and chain, dragging away some blackened tree trunks that had been toppled by the wind and would interfere with spring plowing. As he was applying all his strength to the brute resistance of one particular log, a spasm of pain shot through his back, causing him to utter a sharp oathless Ah!

He rested a moment and was able to continue. But the sprain was deceptive. Like a seed dropped in the ground, it lay dormant until spring, then put forth its leaves and branches. First soreness in the small of the back, then numbness in the legs and feet, and, before the season was far advanced, daily stiffness, muscle spasms, and vertigo. Week after week, deep into summer the symptoms hung on, debilitating and demoralizing. One morning, upon trying to rise from family prayers, he fell forward and had to be helped to his feet. Soon he was using a staff.

And so, at the end of summer, Mr. Cheever had to be told again to let his Samuel go. This time he did so without protest, though he did not doubt it was forever.

Michael, somewhat annoyingly, took a lively interest in his father's ailments. When Mr. Augur the physician recommended hot baths once a week, followed by a rub of bear's-grease, Michael offered to do the rubbing. His mother did not object. She had never seen her husband naked and never touched him except through his clothes; she had no confidence in her ability to soothe him. Edward balked for a time, but one night when he felt his back gathering as if for an assault through all its length and breadth, he turned sideways in his chair and let Michael put his hands up under his nightshirt. The bear's-grease had a grievous smell, but the boy's touch was astonishingly expert. After that he arrogated all rubbing and kneading to himself, and would ask if the discomfort were here or there, and whether it felt better if he did this or that. He fetched mint and mallow for the baths, applied plasters his mother made and, when she had got through her list of remedies, brought in others both chemical and herbal, gotten from neighbors or even from his father's hired laborers.

But all relief was temporary. Worse, Edward's mind was ill at ease. He prayed God to forgive him for unworthy thoughts, but at times he could not help suspecting that the son secretly gloried in seeing the father brought low. At times he wondered if there were not a subtle spirit of mockery in all this solicitousness—just such a spirit as might be caught from ill company. . . .

It was a possibility he could not lightly dismiss, since he was increasingly forced to leave Michael's education in husbandry to hired hands. Whole days arrived in which he was too crippled to leave the house, others in which pain and insecurity of movement drove him from Michael's side by midday. He hedged him about with admonition and exhortation: when he was sent to work—and learn—he must shun idle talk, not dawdle where tales were being told or songs sung, not let family matters be drawn out of him, not fail to report breaches of word and deed. In short, he must always remember that he was his father's deputy.

Michael said yea, but perhaps meant nay. He was strict enough about reporting his own failings but could seldom be brought to find fault with others. He sometimes murmured that it was hard to be both deputy and pupil. In truth, whenever Edward subdued his flesh enough to hobble about, he saw with painful clarity that he was little suited to either role. He would go to whoever doted on him, and plainly he was well liked—by the plowman who could not teach him to plow, the binder who could not teach him that, the fence-setter, the sheep-shearer, and the rest. Mr. Cheever would never have praised him, as they did, for nothing!

One day, feeling enabled, Edward took him out of his way to show him a sorry sight: Andrew Low, Jr., wearing a leg-iron and working as his father's prisoner in a field. Young Andrew, only seventeen, had been enticed by a tanner's apprentice into stealing some spirits, getting drunk, and uttering profanities. While he was in prison awaiting trial, he broke out and ran into the woods. Indians returned him. Thus he earned not only the whipping post, but also a year of shameful custody.

The spectacle, Edward said as they passed by, was an emblem or picture of the danger of ill company, for Andrew had not lost his liberty until he let himself be drawn into license.

Michael agreed but asked if Goodman Low were not also a prisoner?

Edward replied irritably that the Court had not meant it so, therefore it should not be taken so! He marveled (he said) at the pertness
of the question.

To which Michael replied that he had not meant it so, therefore it
should not be taken so! Thus earning a sharp rap across the back
from his father's staff.

But neither blows nor admonitions could quiet Edward's appre-
hensions. Nor could even a stabilization and slight improvement in
his health. For with that came this: Michael growing taller, heavier,
his voice beginning to break, his bearing showing sometimes more
impertinent, sometimes more secretive. One day he was sent on an
errand to the wharf and did not return for upwards of an hour.
When Edward taxed him, he said he had met Mr. Augur outside his
warehouse (for Mr. Augur was both merchant and physician) and
had been invited in to inspect a surgeon's chest newly arrived from
Boston. It was secondhand but had a lancet for bleeding, a saw for
bones, clamps, a probe, and other instruments that even Mr. Augur
did not know the uses of.

Edward, piqued by a note of enthusiasm, said he had not known
that Mr. Augur was inclined toward surgery, a branch of physic held
in little esteem.

Nor was he—the chest was obtained for a ship's captain, Michael
answered quickly. Although (he added) in Mr. Augur's opinion the
surgeon's skill had its place in physic and ought not to be scorned.

Mr. Augur, said Edward, was more valued in town as a merchant
than as a physician, and often seemed to confuse his two roles.
There was resentment of his attempts to collect fees from his
patients—as if medicine were not, as it should be, a branch of
Christian charity.

Michael said that, as he understood it, Mr. Augur meant on the
contrary to keep his two trades distinct. He thought that the
medicines he ordered and prescribed ought to pay for themselves
and not eat up the profits from his other goods, as they habitually
did.

Aye, Edward exclaimed, now he saw the purpose of the surgeon's
chest! Had it not been a prelude to some mention of the four shillings

Mr. Augur thought Edward owed him for services? Or perhaps he had sent another written bill—as he had done three times to Mr. Cheever after treating one of his children!

No! Michael cried spiritedly, Mr. Augur was only keeping a promise already made to show him a surgeon's chest as soon as he got one in!

When, Edward asked, had Mr. Augur had occasion to make a promise like that? Or to explain his fees? Or otherwise to take Michael into his fellowship—for so it seemed to be?

Michael, turning red as cranberries, said diffidently that it was no fellowship. Mr. Augur sometimes spoke to him at noontime on the Sabbath, usually when Edward had not been able to come to meeting—and last September they had walked about at the fair—and once he had gone to get some spermaceti from him when Edward sickened of bear's-grease—perhaps there were other times—the topic was usually Edward's lameness—

Edward said forcefully he did not like that!

Or more often (Michael said hastily) Mr. Augur would answer questions he put to him—

Questions? Of what sort?

Well, concerning physic mostly. . . .

Edward, sorely rankled by a lack of questions about husbandry, demanded an example.

Well, once he had asked if tobacco were as sovereign a remedy as Indians said—and why, if it were, people did not use it instead of sending to Boston for costly chemicals? And he had asked if a chestnut carried in each pocket would ward off lameness, as a plowman had told him? And had asked if a "pearl" in the eye were a true description or only a manner of speaking—

Why had he asked that? Edward interrupted.

Why? Well—because of George Spencer—but he had asked before George was ever found out! One day when he was working for them on the upland acreage, he showed Michael some sugar candy he had gotten hold of. He said he would melt it and drop it in his eye, and that as it hardened it would draw the pearl out by affinity. . . .

No such exchange with George Spencer had ever been mentioned to Edward.

No, it seemed trifling, or just something arising out of George's dimwittedness.

Yet he had consulted Mr. Augur.

No, not consulted—asked in passing.

Out of friendship to George?

No, he had asked about the pearl, not the remedy!

Edward forbade him to quibble and (resorting to antique style) asked directly: Did George Spencer ever give thee a hint, sign, or token of that sin for which he was hanged, and which thou hadst been duty bound to report?

No, never! And truly, until George was found out, he seemed to Michael to be—that is, seemed not to be— What he meant (he said hurriedly when his father gripped his staff) is that children often teased George to make him turn his eye on them—in certain lights the pearl appeared to glow or send out a beam—and they would scatter in delectable fright. Michael had sometimes been in the circle of his tormentors, but when George worked for them he seemed not to remember it, or to bear no grudge, but on the contrary was good humored and—

Edward rapped the floor with his staff and said he had no wish to hear so vile a sinner praised by his son!

To which Michael murmured that he had perhaps praised the sinner but surely not the sin; yet he was sorry to have offended his father, either in that or in anything touching Mr. Augur.

Edward was not mocked. Behind the conciliatory tone he detected a growing attachment to liberty and license. He resolved to say no more about George Spencer—if harm was done there, it was done. But as to Mr. Augur (he said) there were to be no more secret passages with him, no, nor fellowship of any kind!

He struck more accurately than he knew. Michael turned scarlet—his eyes blazed and filled with tears—his whole body trembled. He did not deserve this! he said in a quaking voice—

Nay! said Edward, cutting him off. The look on his face wrung the father's heart but exasperated him too. He would not be misled by

natural affection. He had not, he said, to explain or justify himself!
Michael must submit!

As he did, though withdrawing somewhat afterward, as if he had
been wronged, and showing signs of a secret Pride which could
sweep them both away.

And now Will Harding fulfilled the Court's expectation. He was a
young man, still unmarried. There had long been rumors that he
haunted with servant girls in night meetings, enticing them out to
his sawmill and persuading them to yield to dalliance. In the months
following George Spencer's hanging, he began to behave like one
possessed of seven devils of carnality, and in the end, like the
Gadarene swine, he was driven down to destruction. He forced his
lust on two daughters of prominent planters. The fathers brought
him to trial.

This time he did not deny his guilt—at least not all of it. He freely
admitted to concupiscence but balked at the forcing. He had never
done that, not even to Jane Andrews and Martha Malbone. They
had yielded like the others, of their own will. They had yielded to
him separately and also together—that was the manner of it! Mr.
Malbone was a worthy of the town; his wharves and warehouses
lined the harbor, his home lot was next to Mr. Davenport's own. But
let him ask his daughter whether or not she had stolen things from
him and given them to Will so that he would let her play the slut!
Which arose not (said he) out of his need, but hers!

Mr. Malbone accepted the challenge and fearlessly went further.
He insisted that Martha be called to testify under oath. He bade her
in front of everyone to vindicate his trust. She wept and said she
dared not perjure herself; she confirmed all that Will had said.
Whereupon Mr. Andrews quickly rose and said that Jane had confessed privately to certain things too—he would not say they were
exactly the same things—but the Court had his permission to hold
her accountable.

Thus Will Harding: thrusting up from below, dragging both girls
with him through the mire to the whipping post. Yet not quite
"with" him. On the lecture-day that his back was laid open to the

bone, the girls were brought to see it. On the next lecture-day, however—their appointed time—they stayed home; and so they did the next Wednesday, and the next, offering one excuse and another until two months had gone by. But when Martha vowed she would plead pregnancy to avoid whipping, her father endured her no longer. He took her to lecture by force and afterward onto the green, where he bade the executioner not to lighten the strokes in respect to her youth and sex, and stood by with his head uncovered to acknowledge his own guiltiness—whatever it was. Mr. Andrews must then follow suit. But whereas Jane recovered quickly and was soon seen again, Martha fell ill and had to go to Bermuda for more than a year.

Michael witnessed Will's punishment—Edward saw to it. And both attended lecture beforehand, which Edward did not always do. Not that he lacked interest in doctrinal instruction, but too often (in his opinion) Mr. Davenport used Wednesday lectures to conduct veiled personal controversies with church members who found fault with the New Haven way. For the same reason Edward took no pleasure in informal meetings in homes, where laymen retaliated upon Mr. Davenport. New Haven's reputation for contentiousness was not, in his view, an enviable one.

On Will Harding's Wednesday, though, Mr. Davenport put aside his warfare with tolerators and liberalizers, and preached another soul-awakening sermon on the attraction of ill company for the second generation. If the former did their work of corrupting, what were whipping and banishment to that? The true price would be exacted later from overseers of the young vines. What though the creeping things were trod upon and cast out? Still there remained the damaged buds and shoots—who knew how many, and to what degree?

Prophetic words! On the way home Michael remarked inappropriately upon the way Will Harding had neither fainted nor vomited, despite the severity of the flogging.

Edward said that was rather a sign of the hardihood of sin than a thing to be admired.

Michael said that was his meaning.

Edward glanced at him sideways and said his tone bespoke something else.

Michael denied it.

Edward said he thanked God he had not had to send Michael to the sawmill after Will proved an evil counselor to George Spencer.

He was not so proved! said Young Pride. That was not the charge—

He caught himself, and cringed as if expecting a blow across his shoulders. The staff did not fall. It was not even raised. Edward only turned his face away and limped along in silence.

And yet, said Michael in a quavering voice, he had somewhat on his conscience concerning Will Harding. . . .

Aye, said Edward, so he supposed.

Not that Will had ever discussed filthy doings in his presence, or ever defended disrespect for the law; that is, not directly—

Edward ordered him to stop equivocating and clear his conscience concerning Will Harding.

Well then, one day in February he had gone to the mill with a note disputing some charges—did his father remember that errand?— and had accidentally overheard something which he should have perhaps reported. Will was studying the note, with no one else about, when suddenly George Spencer burst out of the woods, ran to Will like one distracted, pulled off his cap as if Will had been a minister or magistrate, and fell to his knees. His good eye and his bad rolled toward Michael but seemed not to take him in. He began to blubber some incomprehensible tale of . . . Michael hardly knew what.

Will immediately sent Michael off at a distance, but voices carried in the clear cold air, and he heard whether he would or not. Will said sternly that George must go to a minister or magistrate—this was not something to be confessed to a sawyer!

No, George wept, they would surely hang him!

Did George expect Will to hear such a thing and then hide it?

No, George said, it was not a thing that could be hidden from any man! Soon everyone would know! He had just been to Goodman Wakeman's—sent to borrow a whetstone—but coming up through the back of the lot he had stumbled upon the sow and new litter—

had seen the monster—fled! For if he were not guilty, why had the piglet one eye only, with a pearl in it? And why had he been the first to see it?

Will seemed perplexed and asked what he meant by saying *if* he were not guilty?

That was what others would say! And George feared they would be right—as the eye showed.

Will pondered a while, then pulled George to his feet and said to him carefully that the pearl might not be a pearl at all but some other whiteness, showing why another eye had not grown. George— though he was surely burdened with evil thoughts—ought not to take those thoughts for deeds. Conception did not occur by way of thoughts or imaginings, no matter how powerful. If George felt stirrings of lust toward beasts, the fruit was this panic and fear, not the piglet. Perhaps God had sent the fear to protect him and remind him of the uncleanness of his desires.

Edward listened thunderstruck. And was not this evil counsel! he asked.

Michael said nimbly that it might be, but still it was not the counsel George had accused Will of. It had nothing to do with disrespect for the law.

The note of corrupt liking for Will Harding now rang clear. Edward searched for the source of it. What did Will say after George had gone? Did he dwell on indecencies? Did he—in line with his sophistry about thoughts and imaginings—cater to any curiosity on Michael's part about forbidden subjects?

Michael not only denied any curiosity on his own part but declared that Will had taken the occasion to speak improvingly. At first he said nothing at all; he merely called Michael back and asked him to do the sums in his father's note and show him his error. Then he said Michael should thank God for the gift of clear reason, since it was notable how many in the world were bereft of it and thus in danger of damnation. Which Michael, although he did not ask, took to refer to George Spencer.

Edward said in feigned amazement that he was much surprised at Will Harding's speaking in such a vein. Considering the sin for which he had just been whipped and banished, more of bawdry might be expected.

That was why he had not reported the incident! Michael said eagerly. It seemed more to Will's credit than not!

Edward did not reply but fell into a deep silence. He realized bitterly that he had never expected a genuine unburdening of conscience, but only what he had now gotten: concealment, self-justification, abuse of reason.

When they reached home, though, it was himself he shut up in a room. There, on his knees, he wrestled with a hard but clear truth, and acknowledged defeat: Goodman Wigglesworth would not become more than he was and take his son along with him. That, inscrutably, was not to be. In putting convenience before conscience, he was merely encouraging Michael's strong bent and bias toward fallen nature and exposing his true gifts, whatever they were, to subversion and neglect.

The brand must be snatched from the burning.

So as not to err again, he looked around for trustworthy counsel. He knew where he should turn automatically, and blamed himself for a certain lack of confidence in ministers, magistrates, and elders. New Haven—though laid out like the City Foursquare—had winding ways in regions of the will, nowhere more than among the prospering godly. Their wrangles were what made Edward doubt the absolute value of advising with them. He secretly preferred his own opinions.

Nevertheless, to leave nothing undone, he went to consult with Mr. Davenport. What was his chagrin when he heard that Mr. Davenport had begun to entertain doubts about Mr. Cheever!

There was nothing to warrant action yet—only disturbing portents. For instance, in Mr. Cheever's opinion that the elders were usurping power that belonged to the whole congregation. He was reported to have said at a private meeting, We are all clerks! We have nothing to do but say Amen! Perhaps Goodman Wigglesworth had heard, or overheard, some such talk?

Edward said he had been too crippled to go to private meetings, and could neither credit nor discredit what he had not heard for himself.

Be that as it may, said Mr. Davenport, if the schoolmaster (him-self a young man) purposed even inwardly to bring authority into disrepute instead of upholding it, his young scholars, impressionable as wax, might be thumbprinted unaware with disrespect and rebel-liousness.

Edward asked if that were a present danger?

Some dangers, Mr. Davenport said thoroughly, were not present until they erupted. That is, being "present" was a matter of being "visible." But there were others that could be called present only in retrospect. They might come to light only in the fullness of time, but their dangerousness would have been "present" all along.

Edward suppressed a groan as Mr. Davenport pursued these and other distinctions, only to conclude that, as to Michael's going back to Mr. Cheever, he could say neither yea or nay. He was (Edward saw) girding his loins for a coming battle; he sniffed it, veteran pro-testant warrior, from afar, as he had first sniffed the anabaptism of Mistress Eaton, the governor's wife, who eventually had to be ex-communicated. The danger from Mr. Cheever was both present and not present. The faithful could take sides now, or wait till later.

Edward decided on the latter. These dissensions always seethed a long time before boiling. While Mr. Cheever was still—visibly—a sound moralist and teacher, Michael might be gotten in and out without harm. Accordingly, Edward went round to ask him to rein-state his former favorite.

He was not much surprised when Mr. Cheever also met him with discouragement and quibbling. Was it, he asked, an irresistible drive toward learning on Michael's part that brought Goodman Wigglesworth around after four years? Or was it something else?

Edward replied stiffly that whatever the reason, Michael would do as he was told. If it were judged fit for him to return, he would return—that was his father's part. If he proved unenthusiastic after so long a lapse, Mr. Cheever would know how to rekindle interest—that was his part. Especially (Edward added) now that Mr. Cheever was officially the master for the town school, receiving his salary from the town, and asking permission to hold classes in the meet-inghouse.

Mr. Cheever said he had not received such permission yet, though he now had four children of his own and but one parlor. But he would not speak of that, but of the fact that Michael would be four years older than his classmates—or more, if the difference between childhood and manhood were considered. These differences bred discontent and fractiousness.

Edward took counsel with himself for a moment, then said bluntly that he understood there was a troublesome difference brewing in the church just now—and it was exactly between these two elements, younger and older. He did not know the details, but if both sides in any dispute were willing to use reason, differences could always be adjusted. So in a classroom. Difficulties proceeding only from age and no deeper cause ought not to be insurmountable. Indeed, Michael might learn something about the value of now leading, now following, of exceeding here, reining in there.

To which Mr. Cheever might have answered much, but did not. He too knew contentiousness when he saw it—and some better quality too, perhaps. If so, it was no less burdensome for being better.

Michael broke out with passion against it! He had rendered every help and service he was capable of! He knew not how he could please his father any better if he returned to school!

Edward said he was seeking a bestowal of him that would be pleasing to God, not to himself. He was sending him back in no spirit of reproach but in recognition of his own error in withdrawing him. And besides, it was settled.

That night, after long intermission, Edward abruptly resumed the use of marriage. Esther received him with misgivings, for he seemed to strive with her and to groan more from difficulty than from satisfaction. And yet it was on that night and no other (she later believed) that God had opened her never-easily-opened womb for the second and last time and let her conceive a daughter. She suggested as most fitting the name Abigail: "a father is rejoicing."

Lykaon

One day Euneus king of Lemnos received an invitation to a royal wedding. The daughter of Menelaus king of Sparta was marrying Achilles' son. The father fancied having Lemnian wine for the guests, among whom would be a number of veterans of the War. Euneus would undoubtedly remember that he had supplied the troops (or at least the officers) with his famous wine. If it were still being made, it would bring back many happy memories of those valiant times.

Euneus tugged his beard, gnawed his lower lip. Was he being asked to furnish such-and-such a number of jars free? Not to mention the cost of transportation? But if not, why was he being invited at all? He knew neither the bride nor the groom, and had met their fathers only in a business way. The message was exasperatingly neither personal invitation nor impersonal order for wine; it fell carefully between.

He suspected Menelaus of ambition. During the War he himself had maintained strict neutrality, provisioning both Greeks and Trojans with oxen, wine, cloth, medicinal mud. There had been some resentment of this among the Greeks—they felt that impartiality was especially unbecoming in a son of Jason. Ever since the fall of Troy, rumors had floated over from the mainland that this or that Greek king was preparing to annex the island under the pretext that Euneus had aided the enemy during the War. So far nothing had come of such scares. Indeed, several of the more aggressive kings had themselves gone under—Agamemnon, for instance.

Still, Lemnos was in too favorable a position to be ignored forever, even by kings with no ready excuses. Euneus decided therefore that he had best cultivate Sparta's good graces. He wrote back begging to be allowed to offer the happy couple not one but three gifts. The wine, of course, the best vintage (Menelaus would remember how scrupulously the scribes had kept track of good years). A supply of medicinal mud (its proven uses had more than doubled since the War). And finally an evening's entertainment by Euneus' bard, who would sing a song in praise of Achilles. Euneus realized that Achillean bards were common as geese these days, when the whole world united in idolizing the great man; but lest this third gift be valued too lightly, he begged Menelaus to know that this bard was extraordinary. He was none other than Lykaon, only surviving son of the royal family of Troy. He had been a servant in Euneus' court these nine years, had been taught the art of storytelling, and had proved very forward in it. Often and again he had brought audiences in Greece and Asia Minor to the edge of their chairs with the tale of his encounter with Achilles, whose heroism, of course, transcended partisanship and belonged to all men—

"Et cetera," said Helen, lifting a white arm to smooth her hair. She had recently stopped shaving under her arms—perhaps because the fashion for smooth armpits had at last come to Sparta. The glimpse of moist blond ringlets gave Menelaus an agreeable little tingle. He believed now that he had never really liked it when she was statue smooth.

He dismissed the scribe who had been reading Euneus' letter and growled, "What surprises me is that he hopes to put this hoax over on *us.*"

"Why not on us?" Helen asked. Her "et cetera" had not meant that she was skeptical, only bored with pompous phrases.

"He must know that we saw Lykaon slain by Achilles."

"I didn't. Did you?"

"Well, not personally. But there were half a dozen who did, who even heard the boy pleading for his life. Even without witnesses," he added, as if he had just thought of it, *"you* would surely know."

She understood him too well to suspect a barb, and said placidly, "I wasn't exactly given free run of the palace. Toward the end I was never sure who had or hadn't returned from battle. Sometimes there'd be a perfect tempest of lamentation; then a couple of days later, the deceased would turn up safe and sound."

"I meant, love, that you would know Lykaon if you saw him now."

"Priam had so many sons," she said vaguely. When she was thinking hard, her eyes had a way of changing color, shifting through a whole spectrum of melting blues, grays, and lavenders. "Who was his mother? Not Hecuba. Did he have a brother named Polydorus? *His* mother, I'm almost sure, was Laothoe. . . . Yes— now I remember him!" She did not say that he had been just old enough to fall in love with her, though that was the fact that helped her to recall him. "A tall boy, sixteen or seventeen. He can't have changed so much as to be unrecognizable."

"Exactly my point."

"Well, then, perhaps it really *is* Lykaon."

Menelaus, however, refused to believe it. Probably Euneus himself had been hoodwinked. Bards were notorious for confusing fact and fiction. At any rate, so long as the wine was the real thing, Menelaus didn't care. Euneus had better not try to fool him there!

When Lykaon heard that he was going to Sparta, he merely shrugged. When he heard for what purpose, he shrugged again. As usual, he concealed a thought or two from Euneus. The news, illuminating in a lightning flash the end of his path, had in truth made his blood run backward in his heart.

Euneus—also as usual—felt pangs of anxiety. At such times he was prone to make deals. "Behave yourself on this trip," he said wheedlingly, "and I'll move the date of your manumission forward. On the day of our return, to be exact, you'll become a free man."

"Behave myself?"

"As a bard. I suggest, for instance, that you not embroider the tale the way you did in Athens. These people were *there*. At least some were. They're not like the Athenians."

"The Muse inspired me," Lykaon said provokingly. "I myself would never have thought to connect Achilles' particular virtues with Athena's, much as I admire the goddess."

"In spite of what you think," Euneus said peevishly, for they both knew who the "Muse" had been, "it wasn't just good business, it was also common courtesy for you to do what other bards are doing in Athens. You weren't the first, after all, to suggest that Athena was the protector of Achilles. But since you've become such a stickler for facts, see that you stick to them in Sparta!"

Lykaon intended to. He was even grateful that the temptation of earlier freedom had been put in his way. Perhaps somewhere along the line he would have to fight down an impulse to save himself.

"Is he there?" Menelaus asked, behind his hand.

Helen, sitting beside him on a carved chair in the Court of Honor, scanned Euneus' entourage, which the guards were just admitting. Wedding guests had been arriving all day, and she was a little blurry. But when her gaze met Lykaon's straight on, "Yes," she said without hesitation, "it can't be anyone else."

Euneus brought him forward after the wine and medicinal mud. Menelaus retreated into royal woodenness, but Helen said with charming familiarity: "Lykaon, now handsome you've grown! Quite a change from the usual bard."

"From the usual prince, you might have said," Menelaus growled.

"Oh, that goes *without* saying," she replied amiably.

"Indeed, madam," said Lykaon, "what court these days doesn't have former royalty tending the children, keeping accounts, even advising on arms?"

Euneus saw that Menelaus' reserve would not last; he said roundly, "Not all conquered princes are as lucky as you, my boy. Some are—and deserve to be—sweating under the lash as they raise stone blocks into just such magnificent palaces as this."

"A son of Jason would never treat a son of Priam so," Lykaon said with a smile.

"Still," Menelaus put in, "he might set him to singing the praises of the son of Peleus."

"The praise of Achilles, sire, is a commodity, like my master's wine; or a labor, like hauling stones. I didn't invent it."

Menelaus hitched forward in his chair. Helen put a white hand on his arm and said lightly, "He only means, my lord, that bards aren't necessarily responsible for their songs, not that the praise of Achilles is an ignoble task."

"Just so, my lord! Thank you, my lady!" Euneus cried gratefully, and plucked Lykaon back.

He sent for him later in his quarters. "Have I mentioned your freedom?"

"Several times."

"The Trojan War is over. Don't let the sight of that redheaded fool Menelaus bring it all back."

"Am I not supposed to bring it back . . . with my song?"

"Not *per se*," said Euneus, pulling his beard nervously. "The old war spirit, yes; but not the old war. Menelaus is itching for a fresh adventure. Can't you see it? There are signs of it everywhere. Bronze ready for issue to the smiths. Tablets of operational strength from Spartan outposts. A dozen things." For he was a wonder around storerooms, archives, and prattling chief stewards. "And why," he asked only half aloud, "are there so many Dorians about? Everyone else keeps them at arm's length. Is Menelaus working on an alliance? But against whom? His former allies? Perhaps he's trying to lull the Dorians . . . or is it to impress them?"

Since these questions were not about Menelaus' principles but only about his intentions, they could not be answered. "Whatever it is," Euneus said meaningfully, "I don't care to be his victim. Let's do our job and put Sparta behind us. Did I mention your freedom? . . ."

"She can't wait," breathed Hermione. She and her betrothed stood in the shadows as an old woman led Lykaon to Helen's chambers.

"What does she expect to find out?" Neoptolemus wondered.

But Hermione, though she always suspected far-reaching conspiracy on the part of her elders, was never sure of the details. She usually had to answer as she did now: "I don't know, but *something's* going on."

Neoptolemus nodded thoughtfully. He had never made any effort
to be like his father. On the contrary, his determination to go his
own way had led him to positively cultivate a lack of physical pre-
possessingness. He was scrawny, beardless, wore his hair short, went
about unarmed, mumbled when he spoke. The very sight of him
repelled Menelaus. Hermione, however, was unaccountably stricken
with him and threatened to kill herself, go mad, or run away in
men's clothing if forced to marry anyone else. She had an ally she
didn't want in her mother. Helen privately took the view that they
deserved each other, for Hermione refused to do so much as
lengthen the too-round eyes in her too-round face, and the front of
her dress was as likely as not to be spotted with wine. But principally
Helen did not propose to turn a harmless eccentric into a dangerous
lunatic, as her sister had done. "No more Electras, please," she said
to Menelaus. He was persuaded.

Neoptolemus now believed that he saw what was going on in
Helen's chambers, or, more important, in her mind. "This bard is
an imposter. She wants to let him know secretly that they'll play his
game."

"They? Father too?"

"Naturally. I've never believed the story that he ordered Lemnian
wine just for our wedding, and that Euneus 'volunteered' to bring a
Trojan bard. Your father planned the whole thing. It's part of his
effort to create a new militarism."

"Using *your* father as a symbol. . . ." Hermione was breathless
with the enormity of it."

"Not that he would object," Neoptolemus said bitterly.

"How sick it all is!"

Once again they were gripped with sudden passion for each other,
and slipped off to commit the act that pleased them no less than it
always did for making their coming wedding ceremony superfluous.

"Well, Lykaon," Helen said, "so we meet again."

That was so unworthy of her that she instantly understood and
forgave his impudent grin. "Ah well," she smiled, "now that I'm
older I find it more comforting to make fatuous remarks. It allows

both parties some leeway. You know, Lykaon, my most casual relationships used to be so . . . emotional and direct. One wouldn't keep that up even if one could."

She waved him to an upholstered stool, then raised an arm to touch her hair. Her loose, heavily embroidered half-sleeve slid deliciously off the round white upper arm. Lykaon shifted his gaze to the wall behind her, but the brilliant frescoes of birds, beasts, and plants only set her off. She had to be faced.

"I wish we were meeting under conditions more favorable to you," she said. "But perhaps you've noticed that your room isn't in the servants' quarters."

"I did notice, but thought maybe there were Trojans among your slaves who'd resent me. Dead birds don't sing."

"No, it's exactly as Euneus said: Achilles has transcended partisanship. The Trojans are quite proud to have been defeated by him. It would be another matter if you were here to praise Odysseus."

He didn't answer. She went on: "But I didn't bring you here to talk about Achilles. I want to hear about *you*. Everyone was sure you'd been killed."

"Hearing the story twice might bore you."

"I'm not asking you for the official version."

He looked into her eyes, saw the color shift, and doubted that he could trust her. It was tempting, though, to talk about himself. He aimed at a neutral tone. "No one in the War has a story separate from Achilles, least of all me. The War was hardly over before people reduced it to a demonstration of Achilles' heroism, a testing ground for *his* honor, a springboard for *his* fame. A man like that needs scope; a war like that gives it."

Helen made a little mouth. "Yes, even in Egypt, where Menelaus and I spent some time, the Trojan War might as well have been the Achillean War."

"Not many people want to hear how the Greeks and Trojans came to blows over a tax on ships—especially now that both sides have lost the sea lanes they fought over."

Helen smiled. "So the Phoenicians are the true victors?"

"Even the Phoenicians are fascinated by Achilles. I think Euneus first got the idea of training me as a bard from them," he mused. "They often used to put in at Lemnos. But it could have been from anyone he was doing business with. As soon as word got around that a veteran of the War was in his service, the questions would begin. Had I ever met Achilles? What was he really like?"

"And who could answer better than you?" said Helen, her smile more subtly encouraging.

"I'm talking too much," he thought, even as he said aloud, "It was Euneus who made it official, to use your word. The first time Achilles sold me to him, he tried to train me as a clerk. I was so inept that he was glad to let me be ransomed. Then when I met Achilles again and was left for dead, slavers picked me out of the reeds and took me straight back to Lemnos; it was always their first stop. Euneus didn't bat an eye when he saw me, for fear of running the price up. The slavers didn't know who I was, only that I was young and strong enough to recover. Euneus, though, saw a second ransom in prospect. He got me for a silver ring. As soon as the slavers left, I had the pleasure of telling him the painful news that Hector had been killed, that Troy would fall, that my father could no longer afford such luxuries as ransom."

"How chagrined he must have been!"

"Less than he would have been if he'd paid more. Even so, he was determined to get his money's worth, so back I went to the clay tablets. I told him to send me to the mud pits and be done with it. I had no talent for totting up jars of wine and lengths of cloth. But he went on trying for two whole years. I think his real purpose was to convince me that a love of trade was honorable—for a son of Jason, or Priam, or any other prince. I never disputed that, only my fitness for it."

"And then our enterprising friend discovered the market for Achilles, is that it?" she said with dazzling marksmanship.

"He called me in one day and pointed to an old man who'd been a professional bard. He was to help me put my experience into tolerable verse."

"You refused."

"I said it would be infamous to celebrate the man who had done more than anyone else to destroy my city."

"Ah! But he had an answer."

"He said that Achilles had actually tried to stop the fighting before Troy fell, that he had been in love with my sister Polyxena and tried to arrange a truce."

"There *was* a story to that effect."

"Oh yes, and others too—all to the same effect: Achilles was not an ordinary enemy. It wouldn't be a disgrace to praise him."

"That, surely, wasn't what persuaded you?"

"No."

"What, then?"

He was silent a moment before he answered: "Freedom at the end of seven years." He smiled ironically. "Counting of course from the time when I could first perform creditably. That wasn't right away! The problem wasn't the lyre or the versifying, but the intractability of the experience. Who would think that being first sold into slavery and then flung nearly decapitated into a river would someday count as an enviable acquaintance with a man? But that's the way things worked out."

"Fate has a sense of humor," Helen said. "I've always thought so. Well then, you did arrive at a satisfactory Song of Achilles?"

"Yes, lady."

"And once you did—or now that you have—do you, bardlike, introduce variations for one reason or another?"

Her tone was casual, but her eyes were changeable as the sea. He said cautiously, "Seldom, and then only in details. I have a few variations for particular places—Athens, for example, where the people claim to be the only true natives of the peninsula, more Greek than the rest of you."

"Indeed, they proved their difference by not going to the War," she said. But she was not interested in Athens. "Do you have a variation for us?" she asked suddenly.

"No, lady."

"There is a variation that's appropriate . . . if only you knew it."

"In Sparta I'm especially commanded not to take chances. Spartan taste in heroes is conservative, I hear."

"Besides, your freedom is at stake," she murmured; then shrugged prettily. "Oh well, some day someone will come along who'll—" she paused just perceptibly "—who'll be able to keep me awake during these Songs of Achilles."

He had a sudden impulse to trust her—at least so far as to say, "I promise you, lady, that my song will have you leaning forward in your chair . . . if I'm allowed to finish it."

She raised her brows quizzically but did not pretend to think the matter over too long. "I'm intrigued," she said, giving him her hand. "I shall certainly do all I can to see that you're not interrupted."

He could have fallen in love with her all over again. It disturbed him somehow, this impression that she now had other goals than that. Even more disturbing, the impression that he was nevertheless still included.

The palace had no banqueting hall. Menelaus preferred to entertain in the old-fashioned way, in the throne room itself. It was small, but any overflow could be accommodated in the adjoining Hall of Honor. A little vestibule for the guards separated the two rooms and prevented them from being continuous, even when both sets of sliding doors had been pushed back—an arrangement which was both awkward and useful, for a guest might with equal ease be snubbed accidentally or by design.

Menelaus was not, strictly speaking, concerned with which sort of snub had been given to Euneus. The fellow deserved a reminder that his mercantilism was too obvious in a prince. But the evening on which his bard was to perform hardly seemed the time to put him out with minor officials, second-string Dorians, and a passel of ladies-in-waiting and opportunistic young bachelors whose tightly clinched waists would not prevent them from drinking a great deal and becoming indecent. Helen insisted that Euneus' isolation was all a harmless error, and had dealt with it in her own way. Even now

Menelaus caught a glimpse of an attractive young widow toward whom Euneus was leaning attentively. Her husband, alas, had died not long ago, and her sighs were making the pendant of her necklace tumble and wink between her high smooth breasts.

Of more concern to Menelaus was the spectacle of Hermione and Neoptolemus huddling together on plain stools that left them lower than the other guests. He and Helen sat on decorated chairs of ordinary height, but he had taken care to wear a tall gold diadem. Helen owned one to match it but had elected on this occasion to make a diadem of her own hair, eschewing the ringlets, curls, and braids of the court ladies in favor of a simple lofty upsweep of natural gold. In addition she wore a gown, modestly cut, of finest white Egyptian linen, as far removed as might be from the multi-colored flounces and ruffles, the exposed shoulders and bosoms of the other ladies. This last, however, was nothing new. Ever since their return from Troy, Menelaus had noticed Helen's growing fondness for white draperies. He had also noticed the court ladies' silent but unanimous resistance to her taste, where ordinarily the queen's fashions would have been aped. Since he had seen her naked and therefore seldom saw her clothed, he usually did not care how she dressed. But he detected something that pleased him in this latest fancy of hers: political advantage. A queen could be imitated; a goddess could not. It was as if Helen meant to put herself, and thus the throne, beyond criticism.

For there had been talk when she went to Troy on a visit and pleaded first one excuse, then another for not coming home. Menelaus had never warned her that she would be trapped in a siege if she kept prolonging her stay in that doomed city. The omission was Agamemnon's idea—her presence would lull the Trojans into a false sense of security; they were too idealistic to suppose that a man would besiege a city in which so precious a wife was trapped.

Rumors flew, of course, about Helen and Prince Paris. Her trip to Troy had followed his to Sparta rather too closely. Menelaus shrugged off such talk. Two more natural targets for scandal could not be imagined. The only thing that really bothered him was the possibility that he might be thought of as storming Troy in the ridiculous guise of a cuckolded husband.

When he brought Helen home, he was annoyed to find the innuendoes and smiles behind hands reviving—or continuing. And he was driven at last to tell her the truth: by allowing her to stay in Troy, he had irreparably damaged her reputation. He offered to say so in public. But since that would only have converted loose common knowledge into hard-and-fast common knowledge, she would not permit it. Instead, extraordinarily intuitive or consciously clever as always, she began to dress in a manner that suggested the Moon: a wanderer perhaps, but hardly unchaste. Ladies who said that her radiant fashions were perfect for *her* but wrong for anyone else found themselves condemned out of their own mouths. Her critics were put in the galling position of having to consider that she was perhaps the perfect wife after all, for showing no resentment of Menelaus' dangerous, even dishonorable use of her. He was the betrayer, not she; yet never in their marriage had she seemed more devoted to him or more oblivious to mortal opinion. Menelaus toyed with the conceit that the two of them were (or in time might be regarded as) the Sun and Moon. Oriental? Well, but these identifications, if not too literal, never did any harm.

His satisfaction with her indeed would have been complete had he been sure that the white gowns, the silver and iron ornaments, the shining coiffures were not simple vanity, a desire to be personally unique with no thought of political advantage, no idea of dramatizing the indissoluble and the symbolic in their marriage. With Helen there was always an opposite possibility. He did not dare ask.

Momentarily disgruntled by this turn in his thoughts, he fell upon Hermione. She had squatted on the floor like a slave while she ate, good! but while her bridegroom's father was being celebrated, she and Neoptolemus *would* sit in chairs beside himself and Helen. His tone and his look brooked no disobedience. The young couple rose and waited sulkily while servants put their chairs in place.

Menelaus felt better. He turned to Helen and said gallantly, "Your new iron necklace, my dear, is not only becoming but clever, with Dorians in the room."

He realized too late that he was testing her. She replied graciously, "Thank you, my lord, for noticing. I was in some doubt."

"Doubt? As to whether it was becoming?"

"My lord?"

"That doubt could never be, of course!" he said hastily. "You meant doubt as to whether the Dorians would think we value their metal much or little—I mean, since we make ladies' things of it," he added compulsively.

Helen touched the necklace. "The Dorians would never know from the design, I suppose, that the necklace is Hittite."

"No, my love," he said, and raised her hand to his lips without exactly knowing why.

Instead of the vision of her white body that usually flashed through his mind when he touched her, he suddenly saw an ironclad Dorian warrior. He sat back troubled and signaled the bard to enter. "Sing with feeling," he admonished Lykaon silently, "of Achilles' invincible bronze!"

Lykaon was garbed in an ankle-length smock embroidered around the neck and sleeves, girdled below with bands of blue, red, and yellow fringe. Helen's gift. It was basically quite proper for a slave, yet Lykaon looked like nothing so much as a prince in disguise. He did not sit down nor, standing, did he remain in one spot; he moved about, carrying his lyre, directing his song now here, now there, occasionally using a gesture or change of posture to dramatize the words. It was a style that was something of a fashion in Athens, where people were not hidebound—or where they were always running after novelty, depending upon one's point of view. It struck Menelaus as undignified, but the younger courtiers found it exciting. Euneus had simply seen in it a useful way for Lykaon to disguise his inadequacies as a bard, which, to tell the truth, were many.

Now he struck he lyre and began: "Achilles is my theme! Help me, goddess, to answer truly, what was the son of Peleus really like?

"The feud with Agamemnon King of Men had ended. The death of Patroclus had brought Achilles back into battle, that and the mankiller's thirst for fame. As he buckled on his armor, he made a frightful vow: 'Not one of all the sons of Priam will be alive tomorrow!'

"The Trojans, massing for battle on the plain, saw his shield and helmet flash fire as he strode among the Greeks. No mistaking that resplendent figure! Hector, slayer of Patroclus, moved among his men too, trying to ward off panic: 'Achilles is a mortal man and must die. As to the day, this could be it! Perhaps you, Imphition—or you, Demoleon—or you, Hippodamas, you will be the instrument of Fate. For myself, I pray the gods to let me be the man!'

"Soon all the plain rang with the clash of brazen arms. Achilles made straight for the center of the Trojan lines, hewing a path of destruction. Imphition . . . Demoleon . . . Hippodamas—who can tell the names of all that fought well and died? Among them, Polydamas, Priam's youngest son, spitted navel to backbone on Achilles' javelin.

"Before his murderous onslaught the Trojans broke ranks and fled, some across the plain to the city, some toward the River, where they plunged pell-mell into the current. Achilles followed these; he stalked the bank, often leaping in to dye the water red. The River pitied some and carried them downstream, where they meant to scramble out and circle back to save their friends. They should have known that Achilles, hungering for death as fire hungers for brush, would be on hand to meet them.

"The first to crawl out dripping, weaponless, without a helmet, was Lykaon, since Polydamas' death the youngest son of Priam. Achilles stopped in his tracks—he thought he saw a ghost! Twelve months before, in a night raid, he had captured this very lad in Priam's orchard where, with five companions, he was cutting saplings to make chariot rails. Before daylight he had shipped Lykaon off to Lemnos as a slave. The price—one hundred oxen—to be shipped back by night. The others went to pirates for cash in hand. Prisoners taken in the dark—profits not accounted for to Agamemnon."

Scattered gaffaws, chiefly Dorian, broke out in appreciation of Achilles' cunning, but Menelaus drew his brows together lest anyone think he approved of his brother's being cheated.

"While Achilles was dealing with the pirates, he left Lykaon in his tent, and Patroclus set out bread and wine. Because Patroclus seemed as kind as reputation said he was, Lykaon spoke: 'Persuade Achilles to let my father ransom my friends and me.' Patroclus had his eyes on the door: 'Can Priam still afford such luxuries?' 'Speak to him, my Lord Patroclus! People say he loves you better than his wife, better than his parents!' 'No,' he said, 'it is I who love, he who does the persuading and prevailing. I would not oppose him though it led to my death. I suffer him gladly; so should you.' Then Lykaon fell silent, seeing that conversation between slaves was useless.

"On Lemnos King Euneus paid Achilles' price—then tempted his displeasure. He let word get around of where Lykaon was. He got as ransom—three hundred oxen."

There were more guffaws, but mixed this time with grumbling and coughing. Neoptolemus began to look interested. Helen scanned the faces of guests who were gradually crowding in from the Hall of Honor. She had hoped Euneus would be off someplace admiring the little widow's pendant at closer range, but he suddenly bobbed up, turning his head and straining to hear.

"For eleven days Lykaon rejoiced in reunion with his family. On the twelfth he disobeyed his father and returned to battle. Then it was that he found himself on all fours on the riverbank, while Achilles' surprise turned to wrath: 'What's this—some trumped-up miracle? Aren't you the puppy I sent by ship to Lemnos? And have you returned by water, like a shade rising out of the West, to mock me? Foolhardy runaway!—for I know Euneus would never send or sell you back. If all the Trojans I've sold took a hint from you, I'd soon be a laughingstock. Someone should have warned you not to court disaster twice!'

"He cast his spear—and missed. Lykaon, crouching, seized the shaft quivering in the ground beside him, but could not dislodge it. With a fearful grimace Achilles drew his sword and moved in for the kill. Lykaon, armed only with words, grasped Achilles' sword arm with one hand, touched his knees with the other, and cried: 'Think now, son of Peleus, how your ship and spear have both miscarried! Men praise Achilles not because he is a killer of men, but because he is obedient to Fate!'

"He answered with a grim smile, 'That is surely the strangest plea for mercy that ever a man made or heard. What! do you think Fate wants you to live? You, or any man? Did death spare Patroclus?

What you call Fate, my friend, is Luck, an altogether trivial force. Look at me: my size, my strength, a goddess for a mother, a kingdom for an inheritance. What luck! men say. And yet . . . some morning or some afternoon, I too—'

"He struck his shaggy breast, his eyes rolled up to the whites. 'Why linger, then—why hang back? I find my enemy—I make death my goal—here, under the walls of Troy. My willingness to die will be my fame. *That* is obedience to Fate! and you—though Luck has lengthened your days a little—you too can choose. No more pleading, then, no more evasion. Choose the manner of it, choose a sovereign Fate—death in battle!'

"Lykaon dropped his hands and sat back on his heels. The two-edge blade circled in air and fell upon his neck—just here. Gushing blood, he stretched out his arms toward Death.

"Achilles dragged the body to the River, uttering a savage farewell: 'Instead of a mother to wash your wounds and a father to follow your bier, I give you to the River to roll out to sea! May fish pick your bones and seaweed be your shroud! The sons of Priam die! Not one shall live!'

"Lykaon heard his impious boast. Turned by the collarbone, Achilles' sword had torn, not severed life. He sank into the water with a prayer: 'Remember, River, the bulls and horses Priam sacrificed to Thee!' The River heard and left him on a sandbar in the reeds downstream. There wavelets lapped his wound and stopped the bleeding. There, too, slavers, scavengers for the living dead, heard his groans. They took him back to Jason's son! The shrewd Euneus pretended not to recognize these damaged goods and got them for a song. But the gods had robbed him of his wits that day: he forgot to ask how Hector did! The shield of Troy had fallen. From that day forward, Troy had no more ransom for her sons."

By now Euneus had worked his way close. The laughter that Lykaon raised at his expense provoked him, but the insults to Achilles frightened him. Menelaus' brow was dark. Luckily no one was entirely sure of how to take Lykaon's ragged improvisations, and Euneus did not mean to let their doubts be resolved in his disfavor. "Accept this gift of song, Neoptolemus!" he cried in a jovial voice which cut Lykaon off. "Primitive art, as you see—unpolished and fanciful in detail, but striving wholeheartedly to exalt the subject, your heroic father!"

To everyone's astonishment, Neoptolemus stood up and said in a reedy, piercing voice, "Since Fate let this man escape thrice from my father, I do not expect the usual song. Let him continue."

"Continue?" Menelaus said blackly. "What more can he say? He has brought us up to date, and not in a way that does much credit to Achilles, if you ask me. Your father was not a man to stop in the midst of battle and explain himself to cowards."

"Hear, hear!" someone shouted.

"He called Patroclus a slave!" shouted another.

"Shame!"

"Mere lack of polish!" cried Euneus. "Even the best of bards—"

A voice more rasping than the others cut across Euneus' babble: "Come, Lykaon, you coward, tell these Greeks the truth!"

It was a servingman with close-cropped hair and a short tunic which allowed him to dodge the guards that Helen instantly signaled. "Coward! When you begged Achilles for your life, you didn't talk philosophy. I was there, crouching under the riverbank well within earshot. You begged Achilles not to blame you for what Hector had done to Patroclus. Hector, you said was not even your brother, only a half-brother. Shameless disavowal to save your skin!" His shouts continued to carry back as the guards dragged him from the room. "You weren't sorry when pirates took you back to Lemnos. You didn't have to face King Priam there, or see that half a brother fall!"

A confused silence followed. Menelaus asked blusteringly, "Who was that fellow?"

"Not a Trojan, my lord," Helen said in a clear voice, putting her hand on his wrist. "A Carian, one of their allies, a breed noted for uncouth speech and half-formed ideas. We should have asked him to tell us how Amphimachus, one of their leaders, went to battle decked in jewels, like a woman!"

Laughter rose obediently, died away expectantly as she turned to Euneus: "You were saying, sir, that your bard lacks polish. Yet

what has he done but tell the story so as to make Achilles a worthy
conqueror? What honor would there be in hacking at the neck of a
groveling boy? What explanation for botching the job? Achilles, we
know, was as eloquent as he was brave. Though the passage on the
riverbank might offend a barbarous Carian, I thought it well con-
trived to display Achilles' rhetoric, so civilized in its irony, so fear-
some in its savagery."

Euneus, not knowing what else to do, bowed. Menelaus erased all
expression from his face. Not so Hermione and Neoptolemus: they
measured Helen with narrow eyes and pursed mouths. Smiling at
them both, she went on: "Anyway, Euneus, you heard Achilles' son
say that he wants the song continued—that is, concluded"—for she
felt the hair bristle on Menelaus' wrist. "In Sparta at least, we know
the difference between a song that's ended and one that's broken
off."

She removed her hand from Menelaus' wrist with a little pat. He
asked grudgingly, "Is there a peroration, then, to Lykaon's Story?
for though I don't know much about poetry, I can't call this
Achilles' Song."

Lykaon picked at his lyre tunelessly, as if deep in thought.
"Goddess," he resumed in a moment, "you who have wrenched my
tale from its customary track, touching me with divine madness,
making me tell somethings as they were, others as they might have
been—help me to conclude all fittingly. Say why men praise
Achilles, Slayer of Men. Young, handsome, highly placed he comes,
the hero comes! Men love him as Patroclus did—unnaturally! His
sword goes through their bodies on its way to self-destruction.
Inspired by him, they call it Fate. Achilles Barbarian! What-Must-
Be has other faces than the one that turned you into stone and dust.
Lykaon, Priam's son, survives to say it!"

Neoptolemus was on his feet ahead of everyone. He drew off a gold
ring and said piercingly, "Take this with my thanks, bard!"
Hermione set up a drumming on the arm of her chair by way of
applause. The guests, one eye on Menelaus, reluctantly followed
suit.

Menelaus bent his lips to Euneus' ear: "This will not go un-
punished." Upon which words Euneus put his own interpretation:

"He shall be flogged, sire, despite the fact that Achilles' son encouraged him."

Lykaon strode out, but Euneus was gracefully intercepted by Helen: "Since the song did not displease Achilles' son, it cannot displease the rest of us. My only question, son of Jason, is whether material such as this isn't better suited to the lyric than the lay." She turned her brilliant eyes upon a courtier who was known to compose verses. "Wasn't it rather a personal interpretation of events than a true narrative, Phyleus? What do you think?"

"In point of fact, madam," that flattered courtier replied, "the use of the third person struck me as an extremely forced attempt to create the illusion of objectivity. I think you may have hit upon the reason."

A rival of Phyleus objected to sterile categorizing of poetic types, and at once an animated discussion boiled up and spread around the room. Only the Dorians had nothing to say, covering their contempt for literary battles with heavy drinking.

Menelaus could read their minds but did not know his own. Was it a good thing or bad to show the Dorians that Sparta was sophisticated enough about heroes to hear them disparaged? He decided that, on the whole, it might be useful for them to underestimate Spartan character. They would learn to their sorrow that Spartans would always fight!

For a second time he raised Helen's hand to his lips, and this time got a more pleasing vision.

Lykaon's first visitors were Neoptolemus and Hermione. They looked eagerly for signs that he had been flogged, and upon being told that Euneus had never gone in for that sort of thing, they seemed disappointed. "Not that we think you *should* be whipped for your opinions." Neoptolemus said. "It's just that we hope you're *willing* to be."

Hermione leaned against her betrothed's shoulder. They stood looking at him—"worshipfully," he thought, would not be too strong a word. It gave him an idea.

"A flogging doesn't amount to anything," he said. "But to be silenced—that's something else."

"No, no you must not be silenced!" they chorused. "You must go on telling the story in your own way."

"In a stone quarry? To fellow slaves?"

"Wherever you are!"

How dense they were! "Why not help me escape?"

Neoptolemus looked stern; Hermione drooped. He tried again: "Buy me yourselves, then, and set me free. Euneus, I'm sure, will sell cheap."

"Ah!" breathed Hermione, happy to be faced with the impossible. "Too late for that."

"Too late?"

Neoptolemus grasped Lykaon's wrist in farewell: "Beware of Helen!" Hermione repeated it in a burning whisper. But neither of them stayed to explain what they meant.

Helen sent for him three times. On the first she told him that Euneus had gone, leaving him in—or on—her hands. "Not that he lost money," she said, adding charmingly, "Of course I know nothing about business. I expect to be cheated."

When Lykaon asked if he were to be set free, she pouted. "Surely you don't expect not to serve me at all?"

He hadn't, and was more than a little curious to see what she had in mind.

The second time she told him, lifting one hand to the back of her hair so that the golden tangle in her armpit glinted, "We want you to be our bard."

"We?"

"Well, Menelaus has a natural reluctance to encourage anything new, but in time he'll see the advantages. Anyway, *I* want you to stay, and he has agreed."

"I'm not a bard, lady."

"No," she smiled, "you won't be able to claim the born poet's privilege of divine madness. But that's no handicap. I prefer some-one amenable to reason."

"So did Euneus."

"And you served him well . . . for nine years. But times change. One can't go on praising Achilles indiscriminately these days, any more than one can tell stories of the gods in the old way. On the other hand, I don't think you'll get very far merely *dis*praising him and nothing else."

She had, of course, a suggestion for the something else. If he'd been born a bard she wouldn't dare to criticize, but since he hadn't been, well, his song had seemed—incomplete. It lacked . . . well, idealism.

She was not disturbed when he grinned broadly. "The fact is, Lykaon, men did fight and die—bravely—for ten long years. I agree with you that it's monstrous to personify their spirit in a brute like Achilles. But that still leaves a question. Why did they fight?"

"For what ideal reason, you mean."

"Yes, dear Lykaon."

All the same, he could hardly believe his ears when, after giving him a day or two to think it over, she sent for him a third time and proposed as the ideal reason—herself! Or, to be more exact, proposed the redemption of Love and Domestic Honor, symbolized in Menelaus' rescue of herself.

He couldn't get past the word "rescue."

"From Paris," she said patiently. "I *was* the seduced, you know, not the seducer."

He tried to put it together. "Paris seduced you, and Menelaus beseiged Troy to get you back?"

"Yes."

"Wouldn't Menelaus object to having Helen linked with Paris officially, so to speak, and perhaps forever? You know how these things gain currency."

"Oh well," she answered easily, "the world doesn't expect much from women. One might even say that I was exactly *like* Love and Honor—frail, in need of protection, in need of redemption by a strong male arm."

"You could have left Troy at any time!"

"Not at all. No one knows better than Menelaus that I was detained against my will. I know him—he'll be enchanted with the whole idea, especially when he sees how useful it can be in this new adventure of his."

"Then there is a new adventure?"

"Isn't there always?" she asked carelessly. His silence gave her a sobering thought. "I hope, Lykaon, that you're only anti-Achilles and not anti-war. One oughtn't to say it or believe it, but war is inevitable, isn't it?"

"If it is, Achilles is a better explanation of it than you are, lady."

"Oh, *Achilles!*" she exclaimed in a rare burst of anger. "Men like that are special cases—abnormal. They make the whole thing so . . . unbelievable. What about all the others, all those soldiers on both sides of the walls of Troy who didn't want to die but took one look at Helen and said, 'It was worth it!'"

"No one in Troy ever said that."

"Yes, Hector said it, when he saw Helen in his wife and son—what were their names?"

"I think now that Hector was in love with dying too," he said musingly. "We had to listen often enough—Andromache included —while he made those same iron connections that Achilles made. Find your enemy and call him Fate! Die fighting! Life?—just Luck, a suspect quality, not basic. These notions, Lady, aren't partisan. When I praised Achilles, I praised Hector. If I dispraise one, I dispraise the other."

"Ah, now I see how you've reconciled your conscience all these years. I'm glad your view of Hector isn't entirely hindsight. Lies are meant for others, not for oneself."

He searched her tone for irony, but she was—astoundingly—sincere. He said, "Some hindsights are worth waiting for. I've never had an easy conscience. I've always felt that I was betraying Hector."

She swept easily to the conclusion: "But now you simply include him with Achilles. Very well. I don't object."

He warned her off. "The story has no hero."

She corrected him. "The story has no idealism. Listen to me: men must have a good opinion of what they're doing. Soon former enemies will be uniting against the Dorians. Achilles, praised or dispraised, is no longer enough. Helen is needed. Why should all these deaths be meaningless? There must and will be Helen!"

"Times change, you said. What comes after Helen?"

She gave him her hand. Her eyes were a single brilliant blue. "Unfortunately, dear boy, neither now nor later can any case be made for praise of Lykaon, if that's your question. I don't know why. It's the way things are. Mere survival is just . . . nothing."

So there it was again, this time as beautiful as Helen. The famous white hand, as he put his lips to it, sent a shudder of remembrance through him. He heard the bright sword slicing through the air: "Choose Helen—or silence."

Neoptolemus and Hermione, palm clutched in damp palm, looked from the body to Helen and back again at the dagger between the shoulder blades. They had been first on the scene, Helen and Menelaus second.

"We told him to beware," Hermione murmured, not quite inaudibly.

"Of what, miss?" Helen asked sharply. "Trojans, no doubt," said Menelaus.

To please her, and himself, he ordered all of them put to death. He rather regretted Lykaon's murder. For the first time, after the banquet, he had been told authoritatively—that is, by Helen—that his wife had been seduced in Troy. But he had already faced that possibility and only needed a new light for others to see it in. Helen told him he was to figure prominently in a forthcoming part of Lykaon's song. When he asked in what light he was to figure, she smiled faintly. "As an idealist." When he looked alarmed, she added reassuringly, "To balance Achilles, the self-serving hero."

"Is that what he was driving at?"

"He had already taken the first step."

To a man, the Trojans confessed to the crime. Which only proved that one of them really was guilty. They died cursing all cowards. They might be slaves, but they did not believe in insignificant fates.

Helen composed herself and waited. Once in the story, she would be hard to dislodge.

Lizzie Borden in the P.M.

I read about her death in the local papers—it was news even here. "Lizzie Borden Again" for the last time, so to speak.

She entered the hospital under an assumed name. They knew who she was, of course, and she knew they knew. Pure Lizzie, the whole thing!

No other details, only a rehash of the murders and trial. I read just far enough to see if the dress was mentioned.

I wrote to Miss Jubb to say I'd heard. On the way home from the post office I fell and broke my hip. That same night, in the hospital, I dreamed Lizzie pushed me. I was lying on the sidewalk. *"Why, Lizzie?"*

She said what she had said thirty years before in Fall River jail: "You've given me away, Emma." Then she turned her face away, as she had done then, and said again: "Remember Emma, I will never give in one inch. Never!"

"Well, Lizzie, you never did," I thought, waking. "But neither did I, though for twelve years you kept after me."

I finally left her. Moved clear away, first to Providence, then here. Miss Jubb sometimes smuggled in a bit of news—"After all, she is your sister!"—but I never saw her again.

I heard from her once indirectly, when she threatened legal action to keep me from selling my share in the Borden Building. I knew she could have no sound business reasons, with mills closing and property values going down in Fall River. I sent word through my lawyer that I intended to proceed.

But then newspapers got wind of the suit. I made myself unavailable. Lizzie talked: Father had wanted the building to perpetuate his name; she could not conceive why I wanted to endanger family ownership; selling would be disloyal to his memory; etc.

I knew that holding onto a poor investment would be even more disloyal to Andrew J. Borden. However, I offered to sell my share to no one but her. I was even prepared to take a loss.

She refused. The building must be ours, not hers.

Ah Lizzie, I thought, will you never give up?

Reporters became more numerous—the past began to exercise its fascination. I capitulated. I did not have her toleration for publicity. I knew how she would interpret my retreat, but I had never been able to prevent her misconstructions, and I did not hope to now.

She dropped the suit, but not all the reporters went away. A young man from the Providence *Journal* persisted. I could not evade him—my address had become too well known. Yet he was very courteous. He surprised me by asking through the screen door if the *Journal*'s coverage of the trial was my reason for refusing to talk to him: "I've been reading our back files—I understand how you may feel. . . ."

"No, that was before your time—I do not blame you."

"The *Journal,* I believe, was your father's favorite paper."

"Yes. Not that that helped when the time came."

"In one thing our coverage was like everyone else's—there was nothing but respect for you. Affection might be a better word," he said.

"I was not the consideration. Most papers—yours excepted—were also well disposed toward my sister."

"There was perhaps more admiration than affection for Miss Lizzie," he said, begging me not to be offended.

"Admiration for my sister is surely not something that could give offense," I said, "except perhaps to the *Journal.*"

"My erring employer!" he smiled.

I unlatched the screen. "Well, I will speak with you briefly if it will help you."

"At the time of her acquittal," he said, "it was predicted that the verdict wouldn't be acceptable to everyone. Hasn't that proved true?"

"Yes, only too true."

"In all these years no one else has ever been arrested or accused or even suspected."

"Well, that is strange, but I do not blame Lizzie for that."

"It played no part in your decision to leave her?"

"I remained with her for twelve years!"

"You never had any reason yourself to find the verdict unacceptable?"

"My lips must remain sealed as to my precise reason for leaving. I remained with her," I heard myself saying, "until conditions became unbearable."

"Unbearable?"

"And now I deserve to be left in peace."

I paid for my indiscretion. Reporters again descended. For a second time I had to call upon Miss Jubb. "It will not die!" I said. She hurried over from Fall River and helped spirit me away. She is the only person who knows my present whereabouts.

She apologized for not coming in person to tell me about Lizzie's funeral. Poor soul! She's old as I am. But I understand what she meant: if she could just *tell* me, she could make it seem less—Lizzie. As if I expected anything else!

She wrote that Lizzie had an operation about a year ago from which she never really recovered. In fact, she felt so strongly that she was going to die that she made plans for her own funeral and left them in a sealed envelope with Helen Leighton.

Miss Leighton was her latest close friend, a young woman from Boston, not Fall River. According to Miss Jubb, people liked her but made fun of her a little after she took up with Lizzie. She became obsessed with the idea that Fall River had mistreated Lizzie, but would maintain in the same breath that Lizzie said and did nothing to influence her.

She faithfully carried out Lizzie's last wishes: the funeral to be held at home, someone to sing "My Ain Countree," a select list of people to be invited. Miss Jubb was one.

When the mourners arrived, there was no Lizzie—only Miss Leighton, pale as death. She had just learned that Lizzie had been buried the night before. Lizzie had left the undertaker instructions —and paid him well to keep them secret. She had not mentioned a funeral service to him. On the contrary, she specified that, after the laying out, the coffin was to be closed, draped in black, and taken by night—it must be the *same* night—to Oak Grove cemetery. There it was to be lowered into the grave by Negroes—dressed in black. She specifically forbade any other attendants.

He had carried out her instructions to the letter, including the malicious timing.

Poor Miss Leighton! Most of the people on that select list came out of mere curiosity. She must have realized too late that Lizzie only wanted to spite them. And she would have to partly admit that they deserved it. I picture her standing in the parlor; she cannot quite condone Lizzie's action, cannot quite condemn it. People file past her in the awkward silence. She is just beginning to understand what was required of a friend of Lizzie Borden.

Lizzie did not exchange class rings with a friend when she graduated from high school. She gave hers to Father. We had just got home from the exercises. "I want you to wear it always."

Father was not sentimental, but he was always solicitous of Lizzie's feelings. Perhaps he felt that she had been more disturbed by Mother's death than I was, though she was only two at the time, while I was twelve. And she was only four when he remarried. She found it natural to call Abby "Mother." I did not, and received permission to use her first name. A few years before the murders we both changed to "Mrs. Borden."

Lizzie soon found that attempts to treat Mrs. Borden as a mother only embarrassed and alarmed her. From the beginning she could scarcely be prevailed upon to go out of the house or do anything in it except eat. She took to staying upstairs as much as possible; she would come down only for meals or between-meals foraging. Her weight, before many years passed, made even these descents laborious.

Lizzie turned back to me. She came to dislike Mrs. Borden intensely. I did not—I just could never grow fond of her—of her sloth, her physical grossness. I compared her to Mother and found her wanting. I did not, however, think of her as coming between Father and me. The older Lizzie grew, the more she behaved as if every token of affection for Mrs. Borden were stolen from her. She fought back.

Father said he would attach the ring to his watch chain—"No, you must wear it on your finger!" He said it was too small—"Then wear it on your small finger!" He started to put it on his right hand—"Not that hand, Father!" I remember how he hesitated—the least thing was liable to send her off into one of her peculiar spells. Then, silently, he worked the ring onto the small finger of his left hand. It clashed unavoidably with his wedding band. Abby said never a word. I saw her a few minutes later, groaning up the stairs with a mutton sandwich, a wedge of apple pie, and a pitcher of iced tea with half an inch of sugar boiling up from the bottom.

When Lizzie was excited, her eyes seemed to grow larger and paler. Color and expression would drain away; she would stare hard, but at something no one else could see. The effect was not pleasant, though reporters at the trial found it "incandescent," "hypnotizing," and so on—descriptions she cherished. No one found the mottling of her skin attractive. Even as a girl Lizzie did not blush in the usual sense. Blood rising in her face would not blend with the pallor of her skin, but fought an ugly battle all along her jaw and straggled out in her cheeks. Often when these signs of inner emotion were most evident, her voice and manner would indicate total self-possession: "I have received Mr. Robinson's bill. Twenty-five thousand dollars. I will not pay it."

Noting the inner stress, I did not mention her new house on French Street or any of the other extravagances that had followed her acquittal far more quickly than Mr. Robinson's fee.

"I thought he was my friend—he called me his little girl."

"He saved your life, Lizzie."

She stared. "I was innocent, was I not?"

"Mr. Robinson made the jury see it."

"You did not think it was self-evident?"

"It is not a matter of what I thought."

"Well, I won't pay it! I won't be robbed, I won't be blackmailed!"

"Blackmailed!"

"Don't you see the dilemma Mr. Robinson is trying to put me in? No innocent person would be charged such a fee. If I pay, it will be said that I bought an acquittal."

"And if you don't?"

"That I wasn't willing to pay for one."

I hardly knew where to begin. "Why would he create such a dilemma?"

"You can't guess?"

"No."

"Mr. Robinson doesn't believe me innocent," she said flatly. "This is his way of saying so. I will not pay it!"

Either then or later—for we went over and over every point—she said: "You look so downcast, Emma. If it will make you feel better, *you* may pay him."

"How could it make me feel better, unless you lacked the money?"

"True," she said. "And you've had enough expenses from the trial as it is."

"I? I have had no expenses."

"Yes," she said, staring hard, "it's common knowledge."

Either then or later, when I wearied of playing games, I asked bluntly: "Are you speaking of Bridget?"

"Yes. Of the way she dressed at the trial—her ticket back to Ireland—the farm she bought there. She couldn't possibly have saved enough from the wages Father paid her."

"Servant girls may believe she was bribed," I said sharply, "but no sensible person does."

"No sensible person believes that Bridget couldn't recall what dress I was wearing that morning, or whether I had changed from cotton to silk."

"If she remembered and chose not to tell, it was because she did not think the matter important. Her silence did not become an expense."

She opened her fan and looked at me over the edge. It was Mr. Robinson who persuaded her to carry a black fan during the trial. She had never used one before, but so much attention was paid to it that she was never afterward without one. To my occasional annoyance.

"Put that away. Coyness does not become either of us. I will tell you now that I made arrangements to help Bridget financially during the trial. She was, after all, unemployed for almost a year. She chose to spend the money on showy dresses. That was indiscreet, but I was not bribing her and therefore had no right to object. However it may have looked, my conscience was clear. When the trial was over, she wanted to go home—that is natural—and Ireland is her home."

"It's all so easily explained, yet you've never explained it before."

"It was my own affair."

"Oh Emma," she suddenly said in a tone of peculiar satisfaction, "you are not a good liar! You believe I changed from the cotton to the silk that morning! You believe Bridget lied when she said she couldn't remember!"

"Lizzie, Lizzie! if you say you wore the silk all morning, I believe you. If Bridget lied when she said she could not remember anything to the contrary, she lied upon her own motion. The money I gave her was not a bribe!"

"It was a reward."

"It was neither. It was a simple gift!"

She would not pay Mr. Robinson, but I found her at work on a gift for Mr. Moody. I thought at first she was adding to her own scrapbook of clippings and memorabilia of the trial. Then I saw two police photographs mounted opposite each other. Father, half-sliding off the couch, profile streaked with blood. Mrs. Borden, wedged between the bed and bureau, feet awkwardly splayed. . . .

"Where—how—did you get these?"

"I asked for them. Oh, not for myself—" and she showed me the flyleaf: "For Mr. William Moody, as a memento of an interesting occasion."

"Lizzie, you cannot!"

"It's a duplicate of my own . . . except for those additions."

"Oh Lizzie, at the very least this is not in good taste!" For some reason the remark made her laugh out loud. I persisted: "It is . . . inappropriate—it will seem that you are taunting him."

"Not at all," she replied, fetching string and wrapping paper. "Mr. Moody is a young man on the threshold of his career. Even though he lost this case, his connection with it cannot but help him. He will be grateful."

The assistant prosecuting attorney!

That time the house was broken into, in broad daylight, about a year before the murders, the police questioned and questioned Bridget. A little gold watch and some jewelry were missing from Mrs. Borden's dressing table. She discovered the theft when she returned from one of her rare outings, a drive with Father to Swansea. The rest of us had been home all day; none of us heard any suspicious noises. It was Lizzie who discovered how the thief got in. Someone had left the cellar door unbolted, and the lock had been picked with a nail—Lizzie pointed to it still hanging in the keyhole.

The police came back the next day to question Bridget further. Maybe she had opened the cellar door for an accomplice. . . . Lizzie had to be sent to her room, she could not stop talking and interfering. Father had already asked the police not to release news of the theft to the papers; now he asked them to drop the investigation altogether. "You will never catch the real thief. . . ." The word "real" struck me as odd at the time, but I believe he was trying to let the police know that he had no suspicion at all of Bridget.

That night he locked and bolted the door between Lizzie's bedroom and the one he and Mrs. Borden used. It had never been locked before. It was never unlocked again.

I knew Lizzie would forgive Father anything. I braced myself for an attack on Mrs. Borden for that silent accusation. Instead, she seemed to put the matter completely out of her mind.

But a few weeks later, while Alice Russell was paying a visit, Lizzie suddenly began a rambling account of the theft. Alice had not heard of it before, and after a few questions, she fell tactfully silent. Lizzie said Father had been right to call off the investigation. Robberies so bold yet limited in scope (nothing taken but what belonged to Mrs. Borden!) could seldom be solved. Even the police said so. All we could do was try to prevent a repetition—as she had done by putting a lock on her side of the door. If a thief came up the backstairs again, he would not longer be able to pass from Father's room into hers and so to the front of the house. . . .

I heard this in startled silence. Later I checked. There indeed, on Lizzie's side of the door, was a shiny new lock.

Of the people who dropped away after the trial, I missed Alice Russell most of all. She had been my best friend. Lizzie once made the astonishing suggestion that I exchange calls with her again.

"You know I cannot do that, Lizzie."

"Why not? Unless you have some quarrel I don't know about."

"We have not quarreled, for we have not spoken since she testified against you."

She was toying with her fan. "She did not testify against me. She told what she saw. It could not hurt me."

I said warily, "I wonder that you can put it out of your memory so easily."

"Well," she said negligently, "what did she have to tell except that she saw me tearing up an old dress? But you saw me too—you knew the dress. When I told you I was going to burn it, you said, 'Yes, why don't you?'"

"In that," I said bitterly, "I had to contradict her."

"Is she angry about that? She can't be so petty!"

"I do not know how she feels."

"If she wanted her reputation for accuracy to go unchallenged, she shouldn't have waited three months before telling her story."

I could have wept. "Out of fondness for me, Lizzie! When she could bear it no longer, she sent to beg my forgiveness!"

"Ah, now I understand a little better your desire not to see her again," Lizzie said on that note of satisfaction I was learning to dread. "She needn't have implicated you."

"She did not implicate me."

"Forced you to contradict her, then."

"You did that! I told about the dress-burning the way *you* remembered it."

She rose and walked about the room, opening and shutting her fan. "Why did you let me burn it, Emma, when you still believed I had changed?"

According to Alice, I had tried. I had not said, "Why don't you?" but "I would not do that if I were you!" She was coming back from church on Sunday, after the murders on Thursday. I let her in the back door, followed her through the entry into the kitchen. Lizzie was standing between the stove and the coal closet. She had a blue dress in her hand, with brown stains on the skirt. I knew she had stained a blue dress with brown paint several months earlier—several times she had mentioned throwing it away. I also knew the police were looking for a blue dress with bloodstains on it. I could have said either "I would not do that if I were you" or "Why don't you?" Either.

"Alice may resent my contradicting her testimony," I said, "but she would never misinterpret my reasons for doing so."

"Do you think that I do?"

I would not answer.

She was never satisfied if I said I did not remember, or had not been paying attention, or had lost my way in the technicalities, contradictions, details. . . . Yet when Mr. Moody opened for the prosecution I remember thinking, "So there it all is—so *that's* their side," just as if nine months had not gone by, with an inquest and preliminary investigation. Mr. Robinson could bring tears to my eyes, but I could seldom apply when he was saying to the point at hand. Mr. Moody was mercilessly clear and orderly. Watching Lizzie during his presentation, I thought, "Innocence alone can account for that detached expression."

Only when he came to the very end did her eyes and complexion show a change. The case against her, he said, had always had a weapon, a motive, and an opportunity. The real puzzle had been the absence of a bloodstained dress. He promised to clear up this mystery. The prosecution would present new testimony by a witness who had seen Lizzie burning a bloody garment!

I felt my blood turn to ice. Alice was going to testify. Lizzie opened her fan, shut it. In later years, sensational journalism had her swooning virtually every day. In fact, she did so only once. Just as Mr. Moody finished and started for his table, she fainted dead away.

Mr. Moody's triumph was short lived. In the days following, so many rulings from the bench favored the defense that he was rumored to have urged the district attorney to withdraw from the case, to throw the responsibility for freeing Lizzie upon the Court. There was much ugly comment upon the fact that the presiding judge was one of Mr. Robinson's appointees when Mr. Robinson was governor of the state. The district attorney, however, did not withdraw. Apparently he did not feel as strongly as Mr. Moody that the trial was a mockery of justice.

Still, it was not to him that Lizzie sent her "memento of an interesting occasion."

Eventually she paid Mr. Robinson but announced that her door would be closed to him. Not that he had ever made any attempt to call. Neither had Mr. Jennings, her other lawyer, our family lawyer. After we moved up on the hill, he simply dropped away.

The house seemed far too large to me, but Lizzie said she planned to entertain extensively and would need room. She was no longer content with one maid; she engaged a "staff"—a housekeeper, a second maid, a cook, a Negro coachman. "What," I wondered silently, "will I do with myself all day?"

One afternoon I came back from shopping and found a workman carving the word "Maplecroft" on the front doorstep. I broke my silence.

"What is this?"

"The name I've given the house."

"What does it mean?"

"It doesn't 'mean' anything; I simply like the sound of it."

"You are making a mistake."

"In what way?"

"Naming a house will be thought inappropriate, in bad taste."

"By whom?"

"Everyone, and especially those whom you would least like to think it."

"Dearest Emma," she said, "you can only mean yourself. And while I value your opinion, you're too close to me to realize that I can't be what I was before."

"No, you cannot. More is now expected."

"Well, that is my point," she said, and would discuss it no further.

But people who accuse Lizzie of "social climbing" because she bought the house on French street do not understand that Father could have moved up on the hill at any time—he would only have been taking his place among his peers. But he was not concerned with external signs of his standing. Lizzie's hints and pleas fell on deaf ears.

It was the only thing he would not do for her. He sent her on the Grand Tour, paid dressmakers' bills without complaint, stretched her allowance with gifts of money. . . . This generosity somewhat contradicted his basic nature, but I never resented it. In such things as property and stocks he treated us equally, and he praised me where he could never have praised her: for wise management. He took both of us into his business confidence, however. I can recall only one time when he did not, and that was when he put a house in Mrs. Borden's name without telling us. We learned of it only by accident.

Lizzie was extraordinarily agitated: "She has persuaded him to go behind our backs! He would never have done this by himself!"

I agreed it was unlike him.

"What shall we do?"

I said we could do nothing except hope it would not happen again. That was not enough for Lizzie: "I shall let her know what I think of her!" She ceased to call her Mother. She went further; she would speak if they met, but would not talk. Her silences were brooding, palpable, disquieting even to me. Mrs. Borden was clearly miserable, though her appetite was unaffected.

Father found a rental duplex and put it in our names. It was worth to each of us exactly what Mrs. Borden's house was worth. I was astounded by the crudeness of this attempt to atone for his secrecy and favoritism. Lizzie responded by refusing to take any more meals with him and Mrs. Borden. The house was heavy with tension.

He came to me for help. I had always had the room adjoining his and Mrs. Borden's. It was larger than Lizzie's, better furnished, and cheerier, with two windows on the south. It fell to me when we first moved to Second Street only because I was the older. Now Father asked if I would exchange with Lizzie.

I said, "Yes, if you think it will raise her spirits."

But he would not directly admit his motive: "She has to go through your room to reach the hall closet. She shouldn't always be disturbing you."

True, eighteen or twenty or her dresses hung in the hall closet—her own would not hold them all. I said, "It is a considerate suggestion."

"I want you to offer it as your own," he said in his driest voice.

I thought for a moment. "She will not be deceived."

"Will you do it?"

"Well, I will say that the subject came up, and that we agreed on the idea."

As I did. But he did not profit much from the exchange. Close on its heels came the daylight robbery. By then I was taking my meals with Lizzie and had ceased to call Mrs. Borden by her first name.

I had nothing to do the livelong day. I began to occupy myself at Central Congregational. Lizzie was scathing: "You've become a regular pew-warmer, Emma! You never were before. Why this sudden compulsion?"

"I am under no compulsion. I go freely."

"But you can't stay away freely, that's the point!"

I did not answer. She leaned her cheek on her fan and gazed at me poignantly: "Perhaps Miss Jubb is your reason. If so, why not say it? I know you need someone besides me."

I ached to hold her in my arms at that moment, to comfort her, as when she was a child and had no mother but Emma. I had never cultivated the people who rallied round her during her trouble—I did not feel neglected when they dropped away. She seethed as if from an injustice.

For ten months the people we now lived among but seldom saw had made her their special care. They extolled her in the press as a person of the highest character and most delicate sensibilities, charged that she was being sacrificed to inept police performance and indifferent law enforcement, called her a martyr to low-bred envy or political opportunism, the scapegoat periodically demanded by the moneyless and propertyless. Mrs. Holmes, Mrs. Brayton, Mrs. Almy, and their like kept her cell filled with fresh flowers. Only persons with influence obtained seats in the courtroom—and how many of them female! What a murmur of feminine admiration went up when she entered the first day in her dress of severest black but latest fashion: great leg-of-mutton sleeves, ruching of black lace, a black lace hat to set off the pallor of her face. And from one hand (the other lay on Reverend Buck's arm) drooped the quickly famous long black fan.

When the words "Not guilty" were at last pronounced, these same admirers wept, fainted, sank to their knees in prayers of thanksgiving. Mrs. Holmes gave a splendid reception. All the people Lizzie had always admired were there to admire her. How could she escape the conclusion that she had done something for them?

We returned to Second Street the next day. While we waited for the housekeeper to answer the bell, Lizzie kept glancing about. Only yesterday forty reporters or more were vying for her attention, people were holding up children for her to kiss. . . . Now the street was deserted.

We went in. I made a move toward the parlor, but Lizzie walked straight ahead to the sitting room. She did not seem to notice the bare space along the wall—left by the couch where Father had been hacked to death. She was taking the pins out of her hat. "Do take another peek outside, Emma. Someone may be there."

I refused. "It is over," I said.

Gradually she saw that it was, though in more ways than the one I meant. She did not ask why. She retaliated. Formerly she had been a mainstay of Central Congregational; now she said spitefully, "Let Mariana Holmes find someone else to cook and serve dinners for newsboys!"

Reverend Buck tried without much enthusiasm to reconcile her, then turned the task over to his assistant. Reverend Jubb was more solicitous, going so far as to bring his sister with him each time. But after two visits Lizzie refused to come downstairs. I was their only catch.

"Aren't you afraid someone will think you are trying to atone for something?" Lizzie asked with a disagreeable smile.

Her other guess, about Miss Jubb, was closer. If I helped with the Christmas dinner for newsboys or kept accounts for the Fruit-and-Flower mission, the reason was Miss Jubb's friendship. That, and the fact that I had nothing to do all day long—except think.

Their clothing lay in a heap in the cellar for three days. Then the police gave me permission to bury it, behind the stable, with an officer watching. Then I scrubbed the blood off the door jamb downstairs, the baseboard upstairs, thinking, "So little here, so much on their clothes. . . ." Father's had spurted forward—only one splash hit the door jamb by his head—the murderer might have entirely escaped being spattered. But he had straddled Mrs. Borden's body, they said, after felling her with the first blow; he could scarcely have avoided stains below the knees. Yet her blood shot forward too—onto the baseboard—so possibly he could have walked along the street without attracting attention—once he got out of the house. . . .

It was *their* clothing that was soaked. Pools of blood had spread out on the floor. Lizzie's shoes and stockings were spotless; so was her blue silk dress. There had been no cries or sounds of struggle to alert her. Both died with the very first blow, medical examiners said. The senseless hacking that followed was . . . just that.

I had been at the seashore. Alice met me at the station, all in tears. Lizzie was waiting at home, dry eyed. I do not know why she sent for Alice instead of one of her own friends upon discovering Father's body. It was poor Alice who went upstairs and found Mrs. Borden.

In the carriage she said: "Lizzie came to see me last night—burst in, really. I felt quite concerned—she looked, well, distraught. She said she was depressed and wanted to talk to someone. She said she couldn't shake off the feeling that something terrible was going to happen—she felt as if she should sleep with her eyes open. . . . Shall I mention all this, Emma?"

"It will come out."

I never asked, never hinted that Alice should either speak or be silent on any matter. She stayed with us the entire week following the murders. So much of what she told me before Lizzie was arrested is mixed up in my mind with what she told afterward in court. Was it when she met me at the station, or later, that she mentioned a bundle on the floor of my closet? Detectives had been searching for a murder weapon, she said, but they had been very considerate—they had not turned things completely upside down. In my room they had not even disturbed the bundled-up blanket in the closet. . . . I could not think what she meant. I had left no such bundle—I found none when I got home.

Mrs. Borden had received twenty blows, all from behind—Father, ten. He had been taking a nap; one side of his face had been sliced away, the eye sliced in half. In the coffin, that side was pressed into the pillow. Lizzie bent down and kissed the upturned cheek. Her ring was still on his little finger.

Crowds lined the route to the cemetery. The hush was eerie. When Lizzie stepped out of the carriage at the gate, it was possible to hear someone whisper, "She's not wearing black!"

It was like a portent of the future. I asked her if the printer had made an error when I saw "Lisbeth Borden" on her new calling cards. She had never been called anything but Lizzie.

"It's not an error. Lisbeth is my name now, and you must call me by it."

"I cannot do that."

"You mean you will not."

"Is it a legal change?"

"You know it isn't."

"Then of what use is it?"

"Oh, *use!*"

"Very well, for what reason at all do you wish to take a different name?"

She was silent. Then with a curious little smile she said, "I'll tell you—if you'll tell me why you've taken to wearing nothing but black."

"There is no mystery in that."

"Surely you're not still in mourning."

"Not mourning exactly. I have never cared much for clothes. You know that. These now seem appropriate."

"That is becoming your favorite word."

"I am a limited person."

"Then this is a permanent change in your dress?"

"I have not thought of it that way. It may be."

"Well, and I'm changing my name!"

"The two things are not the same."

"True . . . they aren't. You must take care that your black doesn't begin to look like penance," said Lisbeth of Maplecroft.

She purchased one of the first automobiles in Fall River. I had only Miss Jubb's description of it: "Long, black, like the undertaker's limousine." The Negro who had been her coachman, or perhaps another, became her chauffeur. She could be seen every day going for a drive, looking neither left nor right but staring straight ahead. By then her ostracism was complete. All too appropriately had "Maplecroft" been carved on her doorstep by a man from the tombstone works.

I went to her coachman after the unpleasantness over the book and asked him bluntly if he had been a party to it. A certain journalist had compiled an account of the case from his daily reports, court transcripts, and so forth, and was giving it the sensational title

Fall River Tragedy. It was supposed to clear up some "doubts" that Lizzie herself had stonily refused to clear up. Fall River was agog with anticipation—the outside world too, it was said, though the printing was being done locally. Lizzie was several times observed entering and leaving the shop. It was assumed that she was threatening legal action. But on publication day the printer announced that Miss Borden had bought up the entire printing and had it carted away the night before.

"Did you help her?"

"She say I help her?"

"The printer said she came with some Negro assistants. He couldn't identify them."

"Miss Lisbeth know what she doin' if she get colored mens. . . ."

I caught the note of admiration. It was Bridget all over again. "If she changed her dress, you must tell Mr. Jennings," I said.

"Lizzie may be foolishly afraid that innocent stains will incriminate her," Mr. Jennings patiently explained. "But to a jury a perfectly clean dress may seem even more suspicious."

"If she changed from her cotton and don't want to tell, I daresay she has her reasons," Bridget said, addressing Mr. Jennings. "'Twouldn't be foolishness—not her."

"A pool of blood had dripped from the sofa when she discovered her father," said Mr. Jennings, "yet not even her hem was stained. It might be *very* foolish to maintain that."

"I can't see how me backin' up her own statement can harm her," Bridget said stubbornly. "Besides, all I'm really sayin' is, I don't *remember* what she was wearin'."

Mr. Jennings was still not easy in his mind. He went to Lizzie and pleaded with her not to conceal anything that might damage her case later. He was explicit.

She retaliated by replacing him with Mr. Robinson, but blamed me for undermining his faith in her innocence. She was lying on a cot when the matron let me in after their interview. "You have given me away, Emma."

"I only told him what I thought he ought to know for your defense."

"Bridget's word wasn't enough?"

"Bridget did not say you hadn't changed, only that she could not remember."

"And you persuaded Mr. Jennings that that wasn't enough! Upon what grounds? Upon what grounds?"

"Upon grounds of common sense."

She turned her face to the wall: "I will never give in one inch. Never!"

Nor did Bridget, though subjected to great pressure on the witness stand. Lizzie was wearing a blue dress, but whether it was cotton or silk she did not remember. Her steadfastness deserved our gratitude, I thought, but as for bribing her, I might as well be accused of buying the coachman's silence:

"Were the books destroyed?"

"Miss Lisbeth know best about that."

"Did any escape? Were any saved back?"

"She know best about that."

After Alice testified that she saw Lizzie pulling a blue dress out of the coal closet that Sunday morning, Mr. Moody asked me if we usually kept our ragbag there. The question was excluded. I could easily have answered. No, we kept the ragbag in the pantry, for cleaning cloths and such. Lizzie probably got the dress out and tossed it into the coal closet, next to the stove, while she made a fire. Mr. Moody asked why Lizzie was burning the dress if we kept a ragbag. Excluded. I could have said Well we didn't save every scrap! He asked if Lizzie usually disposed of old clothes by burning them in sweltering August heat. Excluded.

When I saw her there by the stove, I didn't really think of *how* she was disposing of the dress—only of the fact that she was *doing* it, and that it might look suspicious. I might very well have said, "I wouldn't do that if I were you!" And yet I knew she had a blue cotton dress she had been planning to throw away. She was holding the dress so that the paint stains didn't show, but it was the same one. For all I knew it had been in the ragbag for weeks. I could just as easily have said, "Yes, why don't you?"

Under seige, as it were, we pulled the blinds and spoke to no one but each other.

"Where are the books? Have they been destroyed?"

"You needn't worry. I paid well."

"It was the worst thing you could have done!"

"Yes—to the hypocritical."

"How could the book have hurt you? It could only show your innocence."

"Oh," she said with an ugly smile, "people are no longer interested in that . . . if they ever were."

"Then this latest act will give them comfort."

"This *latest* act!" she mocked.

"Why do you torture yourself!"

"Why have you stopped sitting on the porch in the evening?"

I did not answer. She recited coldly:

> Lizzie Borden took an axe,
> Gave her mother forty whacks.
> When she saw what she had done,
> She gave her father forty-one.

I shuddered. "You have heard the singing from the shrubbery," she said with her peculiar relish. "You have heard the taunts."

"Urchins . . . from under the hill."

"All the hill listens."

"What has this to do with the book!" I cried.

Her eyes had gone pale. "The book—why, if they want that, they must come to me."

"You saved copies then?"

"They must admit they are fascinated."

Over and over every point! Twelve years of it! What she would not tolerate from outsiders, she required of me: "Do you think Father really planned to give Swansea to her?"

"I do not know."

"He knew how much it meant to us—all the summers we spent there, from childhood on—until she came along and spoiled it."

"I should be surprised if he made the same mistake twice. He had already seen the consequences of one such secret transaction."

"If you *had* known, though, or even suspected, you'd have told me, wouldn't you? You wouldn't let me learn by accident?"

I would not answer. About two weeks before the murders I had heard some such rumor, but I was preparing to leave for the seaside and had no desire to upset her with anything so vague.

Either then or later (for she could not be satisfied) she said: "Suppose *I* had discovered such a plot—overheard them discussing it, say. If I had come to you, what would you have done?"

"Done?"

"Or suggested."

"I would have said what I said before: we can do nothing."

"Nothing. . . ," she echoed restlessly.

"I mean, we could not undo Father's decision."

"We could have shown our displeasure again—more strongly! We could have moved away, left them—left *her,* with her everlasting gorging and grasping!"

"I had no wish to leave Father."

"He had driven the wedge."

"I did not blame him. He could not have forseen her unsuitability."

"But dwelling with such an impasse! Surely there were times when you felt you could bear it no longer!"

"I was more content then than I am now."

Yes, I said to the young man from the *Journal,* the lack of motive is puzzling. But no one who really knew Lizzie would believe that money or property could be *her* motive, even if she were guilty. She was not acquisitive—that is a vulgar error.

How well I remember Mr. Moody's question after he had listened to an explanation of her break with Mrs. Borden: "A house put in her name? Is that all? There was no more to it than that?" Even he detected that property was an insufficient explanation.

Perhaps it was unjust that a kind of obsession with Lizzie grew up right alongside her isolation. Perhaps she could not have prevented it, but from the day of her acquittal she adamantly refused to reassure her admirers. Questions they had been willing to suspend during her ordeal they must be willing to suspend forever: of that, at least, she left them in no doubt. Not that anyone ever challenged her directly, she said irritably.

"Well, they are friends, not lawyers. They are waiting until you are ready."

"Ready? I should like to know one topic upon which you think I ought to set their minds at rest."

I had one on the tip of my tongue but suppressed it. "No, that is for you to decide."

And so the questions remained. "Where was your sister during the murders?" Thirty years later! The very question I had bitten back! The first one I asked when I returned from the seaside!

"Her whereabouts were established at the trial," I said to the reporter.

I could still see Mr. Moody exhibiting his plan of the house and yard. The front door was locked; the intruder had to come in the back, pass to the front, go upstairs to kill Mrs. Borden, come down to kill Father, escape out the back again—all without being seen or heard by either Lizzie or Bridget. And between the two deaths, an hour and a half gone by. . . .

He traced Bridget's movements with a pointer: working outside when Mrs. Borden died, taking a nap in her room in the garret when Father died. But where was Lizzie when Mrs. Borden died? Ironing in the kitchen? How did the murderer manage to slip past her? Somewhere else on the ground floor? How did he muffle the crash of a two-hundred-pound body overhead? Why did she hear no cries, no sounds of struggle? Where did the murderer hide during that hour and a half before Father came home and lay down for a nap? And where was Lizzie when the second hacking to death took place? I could still hear Mr. Moody's relentless mockery of the defense: "Eating a pear! In the loft of the barn! Where she had gone to find a piece of screen wire! In a heavy silk dress! In hundred-degree heat!"

"There were contradictions at the trial," said the reporter. "I mean, did she ever explain to *your* satisfaction where she was?"

"My satisfaction was not the question."

The dress was immaculate when the police arrived. No blood on the hem, no dust from the loft.

She had a telephone installed at "Maplecroft." It was of little use to her and proved a trap to me. She had begun to take short trips out of town, staying for a day, sometimes overnight, in Boston or

Providence. . . . On these occasions I would sometimes ring up Miss Jubb and invite her to bring her work over. One day while we were cozily occupied in my room, crocheting doilies for a church bazaar, Lizzie returned unexpectedly from Providence. I heard her speaking to the maid. I rose without haste and went to the head of the stairs. She had already started up. I remember her fur cape and her hat with iridescent birdwings. Her muff, oddly enough, was stuffed into her reticule.

"Miss Jubb is here, Lizzie," I said firmly. "Won't you come say hello?"

She brushed past me—she seemed distracted, breathless. "In a moment. . . ."

"She is taking off her things," I told Miss Jubb, but my face betrayed me. She started to put away her work: "Perhaps she does not feel well. . . ."

At that moment Lizzie swept into the room, color high, eyes luminous, both hands extended. "Dear Miss Jubb, how very nice to see you! I've been hoping you'd call!" For the next five minutes she chattered torrentially. Miss Jubb sent me so many gratified glances that I was forced to bend my eyes upon my crocheting. "You came back early. Did you finish all your shopping?"

"Oh yes—or rather, no. After Tilden's I let the rest go."

"Tilden's have such lovely things," sighed Miss Jubb, who could not afford any of them.

"Shall I show you what I bought there?" cried Lizzie. She hurried out and returned with two porcelain paintings. One was called "Love's Dream," the other "Love's Awakening." Miss Jubb went into raptures over them. Lizzie said effusively: "I meant them for my wall, but now I have a different plan. One will be yours, the other Emma's, as a reminder to you of your friendship. You shall not refuse me!"

Miss Jubb burst into tears. For some time she had been hinting that I kept her away from Lizzie unnecessarily. I was unpleasantly reminded of other times when Lizzie pressed gifts on people, but, reproaching myself, I said that if Miss Jubb would accept her porcelain, I would accept mine. Blushing, she chose "Love's Dream" as more appropriate for herself. Lizzie laughed heartily: "Well, Emma, appropriate or not, that leaves 'Love's Awakening' to you!"

Not that it mattered. Miss Jubb broke hers while fastening it to the wall. Too embarrassed to say anything, even to me, she made a trip to Providence to have it repaired. At Tilden's the manager was summoned. When had she purchased this painting? "It was a gift." From whom? "Why, Lizzie Borden. . . ." Then she learned that the two porcelains had disappeared, unpaid for, on the day of Lizzie's shopping trip.

Fall River woke to the headline "Lizzie Borden Again!"

Tilden's sent a detective with a warrant. Lizzie talked agitatedly with him, then came upstairs to me and said, so great was her confusion, "We must call Mr. Jennings right away!"

"An attorney is not necessary," I said. "Tilden's will not prosecute you if you go talk the matter over with them. You have been a good customer for many years."

"They have no grounds!" she began, then broke off. In a moment she said, "Well then, I shall go to Providence. I couldn't have taken the paintings without paying for them, but who will believe me?"

"Are you certain you have no receipt?"

"Yes. I seldom pay cash at Tilden's; I forgot all about a receipt."

"The clerk will have a record, a duplicate."

"No," she said, staring. "If anything, it was the clerk who perpetrated this fraud—by slipping the paintings into my reticule."

"But Lizzie, you remember paying for them!"

"I mean he slipped them in to make me overlook the receipt."

He slipped them inside your muff, I thought, suddenly weary of trying to believe her.

Her jaw had mottled slightly: "And Miss Jubb played right into his hands."

"Miss Jubb is not to blame," I said angrily. "Miss Jubb has been greatly mortified!"

"I'm only saying that she gave the clerk his chance to raise a hue and cry against me."

"He would have done that the first day," I said with a cruelty I could not control, "if all he wanted was to have his name linked with that of Lizzie Borden."

She fell silent for a moment. "You're not coming with me, then? I must settle with Tilden's alone?"

"The purchase was yours alone."

"When I come back," she said, "the paintings will still be yours and Miss Jubb's."

As soon as she left the house I found a hammer. I broke "Love's Awakening" to bits.

In the spring before that terrible August, Father went out to the stable with a hatchet. Lizzie's pigeons had been attracting mischievous boys. Tools, feed, pieces of harness had been disappearing. To discourage marauders, Father beheaded the pigeons.

I began to think of leaving her.

The nurse asked today if there was anyone I wanted to get in touch with—just for company, she said, now that the doctor has decided I must not leave the hospital—"not for a while."

I said there was no one, but asked to see the doctor as soon as he was free. I knew what her question really meant.

And yet I procrastinated. For I knew that if I ever left Fall River, I would not come back. Lizzie could not stay away. Her trips became more frequent, more prolonged, not only to Boston and Providence, but to New York, Philadelphia, Washington. But after a week, or two weeks, or a month away, she would return—Lizzie Borden would be seen again in Fall River.

Playbills showed how she occupied herself when her shopping was done. She did not discuss this new interest with me; I learned about her friendship with Nance O'Neil from the newspaper. Inexorably "Lizzie Borden Again" arrived.

A lawsuit against Miss O'Neil would have been news in any case, a popular actress sued by her manager to recover advances and loans. But add that Lizzie Borden appeared every day in court as her champion—that Lizzie Borden hired the lawyer who was defending her—that Lizzie Borden had given her the little gold watch that was pinned to her bosom!

She came home during a recess in the case. I had not seen her for a month. She had been at a resort hotel near Boston. According to the newspapers, she had met Miss O'Neil there, taking refuge from the cupidity of her manager. She warned me in provocative words not to tamper with Miss O'Neil's portrait of herself as a woman wronged, misunderstood, persecuted—just the kind of woman, in effect, that she was best known for portraying on the stage. "She is a gifted and sadly maligned young woman. The manager has used her ruthlessly. I will not desert her!"

"I have not suggested that you should. I know nothing about her, the case, or your friendship—except what anyone can know."

She opened and shut her fan. "As for the newspapers, she is not ashamed to have her name linked with Lizzie Borden's."

"To which of you is that a compliment?"

"When we first met, she knew me by the name I use at hotels for the sake of privacy. I merely presented myself as an admirer, someone who had seen all her plays. Later I had to tell her that the person who wished to befriend her was not Lisbeth Andrews but Lizzie Borden. She said, 'But my dear, I've known that all along! It makes no difference to me.'"

I said nothing. She toyed with her fan. "The remark doesn't dispose you in her favor?"

"Why should it? Such professions cost her nothing but you a great deal."

"Oh, *cost!*" she said harshly. Then her tone softened. "Poor Emma! Some things are worth paying for; others aren't. You've never learned the difference."

"I have not had good teachers," I said.

After the suit was settled, Lizzie continued to rescue her from small debts and to indulge her taste for trinkets and jewelry. Miss O'Neil repaid her by introducing her to "artistic" people and consulting her (or pretending to) on personal and professional matters.

I accused myself of small-mindedness. I still had Miss Jubb; she had not deserted me. Why should I begrudge Lizzie this friendship, sorely in need as she was?

So when she announced that Miss O'Neil's company had been engaged for a performance in Fall River and that she was entertaining them afterward, I said briskly, "Then I'm to meet Miss O'Neil at last!"

"There's time for you to make other plans," she said. "I know you don't approve of artists—"

"I do not *know* any artists," I interrupted. "If I did, I would judge them on individual merits, not as a group."

"Dearest Emma," she said, "I've always been able to count on you. . . ."

I felt a familiar dread.

Caterers, florists, musicians came and went. "Maplecroft" was finally going to serve its function. Only, from my window, there was not a soul to be seen on the street, unless someone delivering ice, potted palms, a grand piano. . . . Not even any children hanging around the front gate in a spirit of anticipation. Their mothers had swept them out of sight.

I tried to help. Once I went downstairs in time to collide with a delivery of wine. "Oh, don't look so stricken, Emma! It's champagne, not gin!" I thought of all those years she'd worked for the Temperance Union, how they had held prayer meetings for her during the trial. She read my mind. "Don't worry, I'm not going to break my pledge. Only my guests aren't used to lemonade and iced tea!"

Long before the guests arrived, I had decided to keep to my room. Anything, I thought, would be better than appearing with my feelings on my sleeve. I had prepared an excuse I hoped would placate Lizzie. I awaited her knock momentarily, but only the sounds of the party increasingly assaulted my door.

Shortly before eleven I crept down the back stairs and phoned Miss Jubb. She could hear the din in the background—the music, the strident laughter, the crashing of glass. "I'll be waiting in a carriage down the block."

I hurriedly began to pack an overnight bag, but now that I hoped to escape undetected, there came a knock. I opened the door on Nance O'Neil.

She glided in, casting a glance all about as if to say, "What a charming room!" Then, turning, she clasped her hands entreatingly: "It *is* Emma, isn't it? I've so wanted to meet you! I'm naughty to force myself on you this way, but Lisbeth told me the beautiful thing you said about artists. I knew you wouldn't turn me away!"

She was extraordinarily pretty. I could understand Lizzie's infatuation with her—that delicacy of face and figure did not run in the Borden family. But her effusiveness left me ill at ease. I thought at first that it was inspired by wine, but soon saw that it was only one of many poses she could summon, with instant ease. Her eyes fell on my traveling bag: "You're taking a trip? Lisbeth didn't say why you hadn't come down."

"Yes. . . . I'm sorry I cannot spend time with you."

"But you're not leaving tonight, surely!" she cried. "Won't you come downstairs for a while? Lisbeth would be so pleased. She's very proud of you!"

"No, I cannot. I am sorry she has sent you on a futile errand."

"No, no, no! I came of my own free will! Oh, I'm too impulsive—it's my greatest fault! You *do* think me naughty!" Here she pouted charmingly.

"You have not been naughty," I replied, "only misused. You may tell my sister I said so."

She ceased magically to convey childlike sincerity; her bearing and expression shed an atmosphere of injured pride and reproachful forgiveness. I returned to my packing, not wanting to furnish her with further opportunities to display her art.

Five minutes later I stood at the door with my bag. I turned out the light and listened. Just as I was ready to slip out, I heard voices hurrying along the hall, then a sharp rapping, then the door was flung open. I had just time to shrink into the darkness behind.

"She's not here," Lizzie said.

"Her suitcase was on the bed. . . ." A shaft of light fell where it had been.

"It's gone—she's gone."

"Perhaps you can overtake her," Miss O'Neil murmured plaintively.

"You don't know her," Lizzie said in a hoarse voice. She closed the door, but they did not move away. "I wonder what you said to precipitate her flight?"

"I?" Miss O'Neil fairly shrieked. "I said nothing! Her flight, if that's what it was, was already planned!"

"She would never have left at this time of night. She dreads scandal too much."

"Perhaps *you* are the one who doesn't know her," Miss O'Neil unwisely remarked.

"She is my sister!" Lizzie said harshly.

"But you've often said how different you are."

"We're two sides of the same coin."

"Don't let's stand here arguing," Miss O'Neil said placatingly. "She'll come back."

"Is that what you want?" Lizzie asked in a strange tone.

"Why, what do you mean?"

"It isn't what *I* want. *I* don't want her to come back."

"Well then, neither do I!"

"I thought not," Lizzie said with satisfaction.

"I don't know what you're trying to prove," Miss O'Neil said in a disturbed voice. "I assure you I did nothing to cause her to leave. I came to her at your request. . . . She said you had misused me," she ended with some heat. "I'm beginning to think she was right!"

Then Lizzie became placating. "I haven't misused you. Emma spoke out of jealousy—because I feel closer to you than I ever did to her—and because you understand me better."

"I don't like that kind of jealousy, Lizzie. You must go after her and explain— Why, what is the matter?"

"You called me *Lizzie.*"

"Did I? Well, talking to your sister—hearing her—you know how I simply absorb things—"

"It is not my name. But perhaps there are those who make jokes about it in private," Lizzie said grimly.

Poor Miss O'Neil! "This is beside the point! We were talking about your sister!"

"I cannot go after Emma, I cannot bring her back. She left me long before tonight. I've lived with her door locked against me for twelve years. I'll hardly know she's gone."

"Don't talk about it, Lisbeth dear!"

"No, I won't burden you," said Lizzie. "And yet . . . I can't help feeling that somehow you took my side when you were with her—perhaps not even knowing it."

Miss O'Neil's voice, already at a distance, faded rapidly: "Come now! Quickly! No, I won't listen to any more. . . ."

After the scandal at Tyngsboro, she apparently did not. Lizzie was sadly in error if she imagined that her connection with drunkenness and misconduct would go unnoticed simply because it occurred not in Fall River but in a house she rented for a week somewhere else. Miss Jubb learned a great deal more than I would allow her to tell me—"If you are fascinated with her," I said snappishly, "you must not use me as an excuse." There need not even have been the bitter climactic quarrel that Miss Jubb got wind of. Those butterfly wings could not, in any case, have supported the burden of Lizzie Borden for long.

The doctor came. I said, "I want my body taken to Fall River. We have a family plot in Oak Grove cemetery."

"I've already promised to see to that, Miss Borden, and your other requests will be honored, too."

His choice of words roused my attention. "I have asked before?"

"Yes."

"And made other requests?"

"Yes, but when you weren't quite yourself perhaps."

"What did I say?"

"You asked to be buried the same way your sister was."

"That is correct; I do not want a ceremony."

"I mean you asked to be buried at night."

"Did I?"

"You asked for Negro pallbearers only. . . ."

I fell to thinking. "Well, I will go halfway with you," I said. "I don't mind the Negro pallbearers, but I don't want the other part."

"I'm not surprised," she said. "Do you remember the day you changed rooms with Alice Russell? It was Saturday, after the police told us not to leave the house."

"You asked if someone in the house was suspected. You demanded to know who it was!"

"That night you asked Alice to sleep in your room. You took the one she'd been using, Father and Mrs. Borden's. You put their lock and bolt between us. We never again had rooms opening freely into each other."

"Yes, I knew what you meant, even if poor Miss O'Neil did not."

"You have given me away, Emma."

"If you changed your dress, you must say so."

"I will never give in."

"I have no reason to wish to be buried at night!"

"Now that's more like it." The doctor's voice startled me. "Let's have less talk about dying and more about getting well. You have a long time to live!"

Well, that is not true. In the very course of nature I cannot live *much* longer. If I die quite soon, though—say, within seven days of your death, or ten days, some such noticeable number—remember, I am seventy-seven!—it will be a coincidence. I hope you will not try to make any more of it than that.